PLUM AND CROW

R.M. KINDER

Copyright 2024 by R. M. Kinder

Cover Illustration by R.M. Kinder

Formatting by Kristine Lowe-Martin

All rights reserved.

LiquidAmber Publishing

Henderson - Nevada

Print ISBN: 978-0-9895034-9-5

Ebook ISBN: 979-8-9987978-0-4

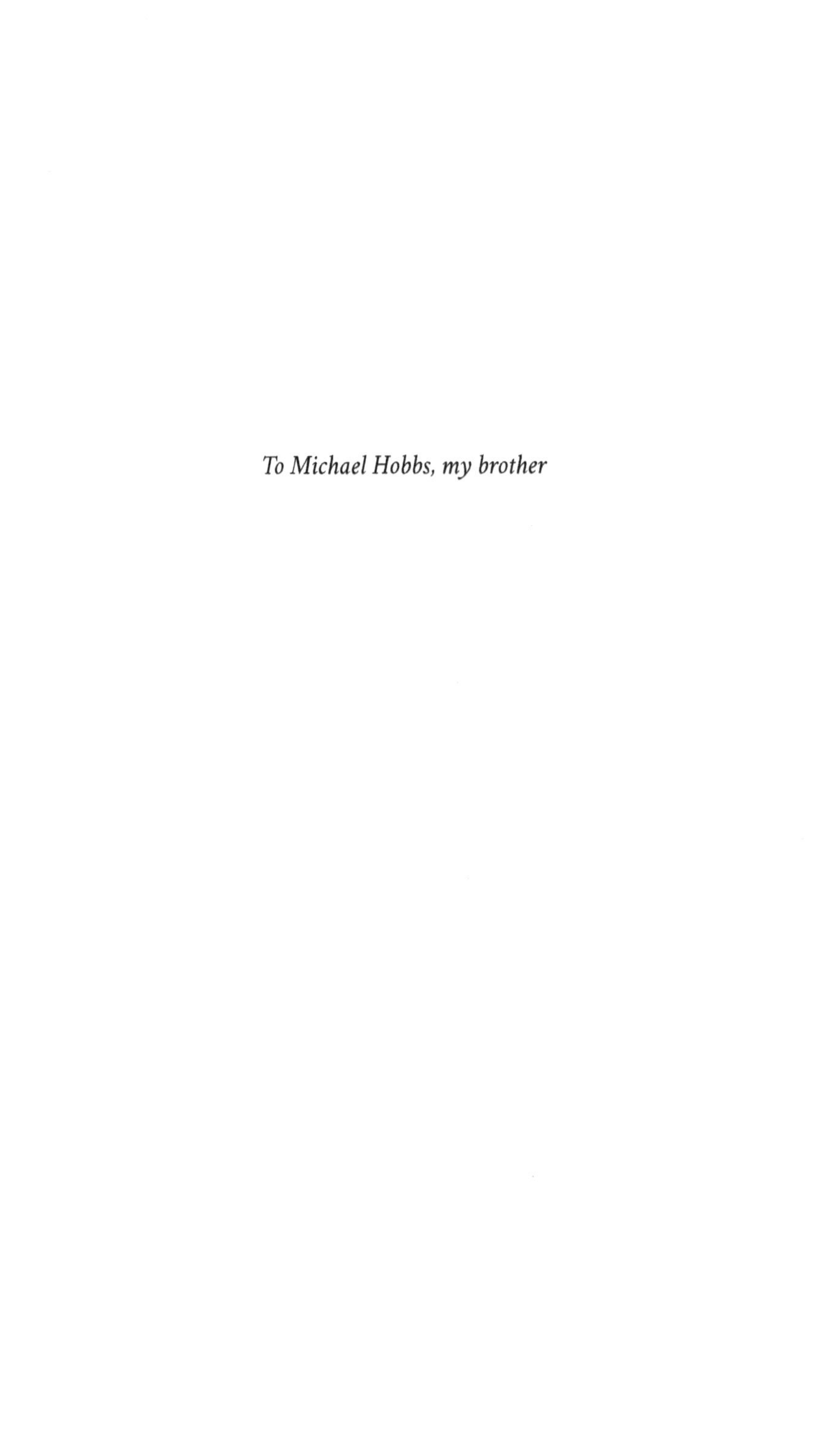

To Michael Hobbs, my brother

"The child first. Always the child first."

— PLUM

"I think we hear the wind and we make it a song . . .
We make the world."

— CROW

CONTENTS

THE AWAKENING OF PLUM

On this nice sunny day in spring, the sky was so solid pale blue it looked like a distant ocean. At least, it looked like an ocean to one very, very tiny person who was lying on her back on a plum-tree branch. She was extremely fair, with almost translucent skin that made her seem delicate and sheltered, as if she had not experienced much, if any, hardship. But the high color of her cheekbones and lips suggested a temperament not totally reserved. The eyes, too, hinted at an inquisitive, alert nature.

Having awakened just moments ago, the young lady was afraid to move because she had not the slightest idea where she was. Only when she heard a harsh CAW and turned her lovely head to see a most gigantic crow in a maple tree nearby, did she realize where she was resting. And she knew suddenly that she might be in danger. She was smaller than a leaf! And that crow fellow was too interested in her tiny self. He was cocking his head first one way and then another. She promptly scurried up, ready to defend herself if it were possible, but the crow just cocked his head again, keeping one black, beady eye on her.

"If you come this way," she called, tilting her head back, "you will regret it mightily." Her dark eyes, the color of blue plums, were quite defiant.

She had no way of knowing, of course, that to the crow she looked much like a plum. She was no taller than one, and since she was dressed in a deep purple gown that belled around her plump little body, she strongly resembled that hardy fruit.

The crow had no intention of eating her, because plums weren't supposed to move as she was moving, and they certainly weren't supposed to make any noise, particularly not human sounds. Besides, Crow had felt oddly comforted by the voice, which was like rain on silver chimes and was somehow familiar in another way—one he couldn't quite express. He contented himself by observing her. Though he was a crow, and she a human, he thought her features were very pleasant. She had an engaging face, round and fair, with red lips, and long black hair so tightly curly it was like whirlpools of silk. He was certain, yes, certain, that he knew her. But he couldn't place her. He sighed. Unfortunately, the sound came out ugly, like a stifled CAW, and he felt a little ashamed. He enjoyed pretty sounds but apparently could not make them.

Meanwhile, the tiny person was talking to herself about how to reach the ground. The voice truly was soft, because all the sharp, hard sounds were lengthened. In her dialect, "I" was pronounced as "Eee," and "such" as "sooch," and "you" was more like "ye." Standing at the crook of branch and trunk, she studied the way down, noting cracks in the bark where she might place her hands or feet while descending. She had an odd desire simply to jump but restrained herself.

"How can I travel down in this frumping gown? And why am I wearing such a thing in a tree? And why am I in a tree?

And where's the rest of me? Surely, I was much, much bigger yesterday."

But she couldn't remember where she *was* yesterday, and being a brave and energetic creature, she felt she had to DO something immediately. Keeping that crow in view, she grasped a slender dead twig in both hands, pushing and pulling and twisting until it broke free, and she fell, plop, on her rump. She was quickly up again, now with a sharp weapon in her hand, one nearly as long as she was, but light enough to carry. She held it up for the crow to see.

"I'm armed," she called. "Strike if you dare."

She faced yet another problem—how to climb down with the twig-spear in hand. She decided to risk, to toss the weapon and follow as fast as she could. Just then a leaf floated from above her. Aha! the miss thought. Now how heavy was she? Could she ride a leaf?

"Well, I could try," she said. "No coward lives long." She began twisting at the stem of a broad, green leaf. When it was near breaking, she retrieved her spear and made ready to jump on the leaf just as it came free. "No fool lives long either." With a graceful, swift move, she was in the center of the leaf, but, alas, she was too heavy, and the leaf too green and thus also heavy, and the two plummeted toward the ground.

From above dropped the crow, WHOOSH, claws open and curving toward her. One claw hooked the gown, and the tiny woman suffered the indignity and terror of being flown upside down. Then the monster deposited her rudely on a mound of soft, bare soil and began walking absurdly around her, nearer, nearer, peering at her with one inky, unblinking eye.

"Just you try," she called, dusty and angry and fearful. "You'll not get a bite of me without a bite of wood along with it." Oh, she was afraid. He was SO huge, and the ground so very strange, with grass at least to her shoulders. Why had she not stayed in the tree? Now the crow was so close, his shadow fell over her. He was lowering his face toward her. That beak could clip her in two! She ran forward, jammed the twig-spear into the feathers at the base of his mighty neck, and ran blindly into the grass forest. In moments, dew drenched her brocade gown and turned her cloth shoes a muddy brown. Was the monster behind her? She stopped, listened. Though many sounds came to her, they were subtle, not from the movements of a large creature. Had she killed him? She gasped slightly, flattened her right hand over her heart as if to slow the beating. Surely not. Surely she wouldn't waken so small and then kill a creature before she even knew who she was. Frustration caused her to stomp her foot and she felt fleetingly ashamed of that, too. Was she hot-tempered? Whether she wanted to be or not?

Cautiously, she moved on, came to the end of the high grass. Before her, past an expanse of loosened soil, were wondrous stalks, topped with brilliant colors. Tulips! Giant tulips. Some had been bent and broken, and a few stalks lay flat on the ground. She spied one large blossom open and empty like a velvet house. She held her gown up as she struggled through the broken, damp soil, and crawled gratefully into the yellow tulip. At the very back, she turned, sitting, and looked out the opening. In the distance was the crow—she could see his head and neck. Relieved that he was alive, but still angry and trembling, she blurted between quick breaths, "Good, you monstrous thing. Now you'll not come at me again. I'm no weak creature. I can fight back."

When no new attack occurred, when the tulip shelter remained stable, she calmed. Her breathing slowed. Flecks of golden pollen clung to the inside petals. Gingerly, she tasted it, and, finding it quite pleasing though dry, ate more. That simple food, coupled with the lush yellow interior of the tulip, lulled her. "Oh no," she said, and sat up erect. "I'll not sleep again and wake up maybe gone completely." But the heat and the pollen—and perhaps an exhaustion she didn't recall—caused her to sleep long enough to dream of rich hills and deep pools. In the dream, she had a name.

Outside the tulip, the crow, glistening blue-black in the sunlight, and quite thirsty and warm himself, was miserable. He wasn't sure why. The spear had not hurt much, and he had managed with the claw of one leg to pull it free. But he felt terribly injured—indignant. He didn't fly away because he had seen where the plum-lady hid and he wanted to keep that tulip in view. From his perspective, he could scan the entire tulip bed. He didn't know when the slow, heavy bumble bees began gathering pollen, but he hoped it wasn't now. They could probably do serious harm to a little plum person. But crows were not impervious to pain either. A bee was a bee was a bee—he, too, could be harmed if he didn't mind his own business.

He felt, though, compelled to stand guard against whatever awaited. Even being thirsty was a small price for the comfort of minding his duty. What duty, he wondered, shifting his weight to the other foot. And what *was* duty?

A human cry, very faint, sounded in his head. A whimper! He peered intently toward the tulip where she had hidden. He was ready to fly to her side. Then he realized the whimper had no urgency. She was resting. It was the sound of a creature in dream.

When the tiny woman awoke, she was miserable. Her lips were parched, and the rest of her was so soiled she could not bear it.

"I like cleanliness," she announced aloud. "At least I know that much about myself." She stood, her head almost reaching the top of the tulip ceiling, and moved forward to have enough room to stretch. The outside looked less frightening now, not quite as strange. And the crow was gone. "I didn't injure him much, then. Well, very good for me. Very good for me."

She stepped to the edge of the tulip and searched the landscape first for evidence of danger, then for the possibility of water. The garden had been decorated with shells, and some of them were cup-side up, filled with water—probably from rain. She could bathe. She could even wash her clothing—if, that is, all flying and biting creatures left her alone.

She pondered her own thoughts. If she could remember shells small enough to hold in her hand, then she had once been larger. That was obviously true. So what had happened? Was there a clue on her person? She held up her hands, looked at her gown and shoes. She felt her neck for a locket but found none. Nothing could be worse than being a stranger to oneself. Nothing.

With a final check for danger, she stepped into the garden and around the side of the tulip. There she tore free two pieces of fading petal, one to serve as washcloth, the other as towel. Then she strode to the shell, losing her fear in the delight of garden scent and springtime sun. She removed her clothing and lowered her pearly body into the sun-warmed water.

"And who is there to see me without clothes? No one would know what I am. I do not know what I am."

The water lulled and soothed her body, and the sparkle of a pleasant day danced on the surface. She hummed a pretty melody and paused in her bathing to wonder about the tune. Did she know any words? Surely she did. She could almost recall them. They teased at her tongue. As she leaned to scoop more water into her hair, she saw her reflection and caught her breath. Oh! She knew herself. Her name was . . . was . . . Instead of her name, the words to the melody came, as if memory were playing games with her. *A circle round, a circle round, a circle round must be, to find true love, to find true love, to find true love, find me.*

"It's another puzzle," she murmured, "and I need no more of those." Worried that she was refusing a gift of some kind, she added, "though any memory is better than none."

She stood, drying herself leisurely, oblivious to everything but her own contentment. Then, reluctantly, wishing she had clean clothing, she slipped into her camisole and pantaloons (the most modest style). They seemed somehow fresher. She wondered how? What were the properties of this new place?

From elsewhere in the garden, other creatures were aware of the pale form. One, of course, was the crow, who waited behind the row of tulips, stalking to and fro, fixing first one eye then the other upon her. Another was a cat in a lawn chair yards away. Another, closer than the others, was a black snake. He had been on a flat rock at one end of the garden, warming his long body in the sun, and was now in search of food. In snake fashion, he sensed movement nearby and slithered in that direction, his tongue flicking out to guide him.

A loud, sharp CAW split the air, and the tiny woman spun. "No!" She screamed, stomping one foot as if her desire alone would stop the crow who was now on wing and descending toward her. She believed he intended to eat her. "No!"

He dropped and she flung herself away, rolling in the dirt, then jumping up to run. But she couldn't run. There, inches away, a broad, leathery face opened and a split tongue whipped and she screamed "Mercy" and fell to her knees to face her death. At the same moment, the crow grabbed the snake by the tail but found the snake too heavy to lift. He staggered backwards, tugging the serpent from the kneeling woman. Just when he could hold on no longer, the cat leapt over him and onto the snake. The crow used the opportunity to snatch the woman in one claw, fly jaggedly up and up, then coast down to the plum tree. In his clutches, the woman reeled at the spinning sky and the nearness of death a second time. But the crow landed on one foot and released her, not too roughly, at the crook of branch and tree where she had earlier stood, then flew back to the garden. There, another struggle was ending in a tie. The snake hissed away from the cat as quickly as he could, and the cat, somewhat mussed up, cleaned her paws as if that's what she had set out to do.

The crow, meanwhile, had risen high, as if establishing boundaries or examining the air and land for danger. In the sun, with his wings spread, and in his glorious dipping and swooping, the crow was not ugly as she had first supposed but was almost handsome. His feathers cast a hint of purple, the same shade as her gown, which was still in the garden and not on her person. After a span of time, the crow began lowering toward her very branch, and she braced herself for his landing. But he alighted so gently that she felt little more than the flow of air across brow and cheeks.

She acknowledged his presence with a slight nod. "I have misjudged you and been unkind," she said. "And I ask your pardon." With a quick gesture of her hand, she indicated her own state of dress. "I ask pardon, too, for this inappropriate attire. My gown is elsewhere."

He was gone. So quickly flying away. He was a bursting, sudden, unpredictable creature.

She could see where he flew—to the garden, to peck up her gown and brocade boots. Then he arced twice in the sun with the clothing streaming around him like ribbons. Was he freshening them, then? A crow would think of such a thing? No. Of course not.

Shortly, he deposited the fluffed, soft garments at her feet, draped over the branch as if laid out across a bed. So close, he towered above her. Even his legs were longer than her whole height.

"Again," she said, "I am grateful." Since those words came easily, and since his stillness made her feel both understood and safe, she continued, surprising herself. "I'm sorry I wounded you," she said. "Most truly sorry."

He stepped back, turned sideways, and lowered one wing before her.

"Are you bowing to me?" Something in the gleam of his eye indicated that he most certainly was not. He repositioned the wing. "Are you offering to transport me?"

When he remained perfectly still, she stepped onto the wing, knelt and crawled up the silken wing to his back. He straightened slowly and she clutched tightly one of his feathers. He dropped down to a lower branch, a broad one, and crow-walked to its base against the trunk. There he lowered his wing again and she slid down, standing up before a hollow. "You found me a dwelling spot," she exclaimed. "And it's perfect, to be sure. To be sure."

The opening was too large, really, but it was now blocked by a feathery creature.

She understood—she would not need to guard at all. Someone else was going to do that for her.

In the next few hours, he brought many things for her comfort: walnut shell fragments, one with tiny chips of nutmeat, another with a bit of water; two early honeysuckles; and enough tulip petals for a wide, plush pallet. He also brought four stone fragments, two of them round, clear and faceted, two dark, flat and smooth. She didn't know what to do with the objects, but she praised their beauty, and he seemed rewarded enough. When he finished his gathering, she stood by him on the branch and stroked the tip of one wing.

"You are a truly helpful creature," she said. "I'll be your friend your whole long life." She sat down. "My own life may not be so long."

He tugged a honeysuckle blossom toward her, pinched off the bottom end, and, holding the flower with one claw, used his beak to pull out the center. At the opening appeared one drop of juice.

"How wonderful!" she said. "Now for a cup to drink it from." She looked quickly all around, reached down the side of her branch and broke free a new leaf bud. It made a perfect drinking vessel, though it would not last too long. The honeysuckle was sweet, perhaps the most wonderful drink in the world. And she would never have known it had it not been for the crow.

"I wish you had a name." She studied his proud stance, his brave countenance. Now she better understood the nature of crows and perhaps a reason for their gathering of things. "Your name is Crow," she said. "It's good enough for your nature and good enough for your name."

He seemed to understand, and he seemed to question. At least he shifted his weight twice and eyed her firmly.

"Yes," she said. "Yes. A name for me as well." She looked all around her domain, the high branches of the tree, the ground below, the garden, and the massive mountain that was probably a house, if she could see it from a proper size. She dropped her gaze to her own self, to her hand and the bud cup she held. "Plum," she announced in her musical way. "My name's Plum. If it's good enough for my new birthplace and good enough for my gown, it's good enough for me. And that's that." She drank a toast to the two of them.

When night fell, and the moon hung high and white above them, Crow lowered his wing again. Though he did not understand his actions any more than Plum did, he knew he had to carry her into the night and was more than pleased that she climbed aboard with no hesitation. He even sensed fondness in her touch, and it eased his sadness, almost made him happy. He flew them to a field where no trees were nearby and where the moon flooded the ground with soft light. Landing there, he waited for her to disembark. Then he began that circling Plum no longer found absurd. The movement lulled her, fascinated her. He shone like a jewel in the moonlight.

"You are lovely, Crow," she whispered. "Most handsome."

He didn't pause. At the completion of the circle, he dipped his head, an obvious bow, and returned to circling again. At the end of the second circle and bow, she felt quite agitated, as if memory were stirring within her.

"You know something, don't you?" she said. "Something I must know, too."

He continued. After the last bow, he kept his head down and she was aswirl with emotion. The moon seemed larger, vibrant, as if it watched them both. A soft night wind rose and whistled round them. She herself was so alive, so wonderfully alive. She held up one white hand toward the moon, then the other. And suddenly she understood. She closed her eyes and thought herself up, up, up. When she opened them, she was far above the ground and Crow was gliding toward her. She was flying.

"Look at me!" she called. "Look at me!" She was amazed. "I could have saved myself all along? Is that true? And you, Crow, knew it." She turned to fly beside him. "So what am I?"

The moon's white light spilled over the land below and she couldn't identify any one place. None of it was familiar. She was in a strange land, a strange life. It was immense, all the unknown, and she was suddenly terribly frightened at the sheer loneliness of it all. She faltered, flight no longer possible, but Crow swooped beneath her, rose. Her fingers clenched rich feathers; she was secure again.

"Well, Crow. Am I a witch? A poor excuse for one, but a witch nonetheless?"

He careened to the side and the night air swept her words above and behind them like the refrain of a song made picture.

"What else," she said, "would wear such a garment and have a crow for a companion?" She wasn't sure, but she wasn't able to dwell on it. A conviction that she had something to do displaced other concerns. "A witch," she said, firmly. "So be it. Then I hope I'm a good one. The best there ever was."

Crow flew straight up toward the moon as if the answer were yes, and Plum gave in to joy. The sky no longer seemed foreign or vast and the earth beneath no longer threatening. If she belonged elsewhere, she would eventually know. She pressed closer to Crow's back.

"If I weren't always so small, perhaps you weren't always a crow."

He floated three slow circles before turning toward home. Plum understood. Now she had hope. She had hope and she had a friend. What more could any creature want, even one as small as she?

When she entered her new abode, a soft light filled it, emanating from the stones.

THE CHALLENGE

The world was almost entirely new for Plum, since her diminished size changed not only her own appearance, but that of everything around her. Now, for example, she was eyeing with some distaste a wee creature some inches away. A strong wind had just whipped a leaf into the branch and knocked loose a cellar bug. "Took a sail you hadn't planned, didn't you?" she said. She remembered, almost, a time when she had believed cellar bugs to be cute. She had enjoyed teasing them into a ball. Yes. That was a solid memory. A good memory. But it stopped there, stopped with the fact that she had once not disliked cellar bugs. She continued examining the one recently deposited near her. Horrendous creature. It had no eyes! Truly did not. Did it sense through feelers on its belly? Through those oh-so-many legs? "You give me the quivers, you do. Quivers." The cellar bug, as if sensing her strong emotion, curled into a ball and rolled off the limb, sailing to a high tuft of grass. Was the bug unharmed? She didn't wish anything harm. She sighed, relieved. The creature had uncurled and was creeping leggedly along. Sobeit, so good.

At that very moment she distinctly felt and heard a muffled tinkling inside her head—not quite words, but almost. She stood up, rustling her dress, a bothersome costume, into position. What were those words? She had to listen very closely and was surprised when she understood. It was not music! It was her own dialect and the voice was admonishing her: "The poor bugs have never hurt you. They're weak themselves, you know, and most constantly working. Something is always ready to eat them."

She glanced quickly around, skimming the branches above and behind her, then the ground at the base of the tree. She saw no one and nothing that could speak. Were these thoughts her own? Was she talking to herself then?

The voice continued. "And who isn't trying to *eat* them, *teases* them."

Oh! That wasn't her own voice, was it?

A few feet away from her, Crow had cocked his head in an unusual manner, a superior manner, and it seemed to Plum he had a knowing gleam in his eyes. Was *Crow* thinking in human words? "Is that you, Crow, I'm hearing?"

He shifted his weight to the other foot, eyed her, then shifted again and eyed her from the other side.

Inside, Plum heard, "*Someone* has to talk to you. You can be a very judgmental creature."

Plum walked a few inches down the limb toward Crow, and even for this short distance had to lift the dress skirt to keep from snagging it on the newly budding twigs.

Watching her, Crow was a little wary, because this wee human had a nasty temper when she felt threatened or wronged. But he nearly forgot his concern. He *did* love looking at her, at the thick sworling hair, arched eyebrows, delft-blue eyes. Perhaps humans would find her too plump and her clothing too colorful and rich, but Crow thought she was perfection—outward perfection at least.

Now, nearer him, Plum placed her hands on her waist, thumbs in front, fingers behind, and threw back her head. "If you have something to say to me," she called, "you would do better to speak direct. I do not like this pretending to be me. It's mean to harangue me in my own voice."

Crow didn't open his beak, but Plum heard exactly what he thought. "I can't speak any other way. It's hear me in your voice or don't hear me at all."

Now she was certain the speaker—or thinker—was Crow, because she wouldn't speak so sharply to herself, would she? "You could warn me," she said to her dark friend. "You could at least make a crow-noise first, so I'd be on guard. Now, I sound crazy, warring with myself like that."

"Warring with oneself," she heard, "can be a blessing."

Though the words hadn't come through her ears, Plum cupped her hands over them, stomped her foot, and whistled. She would listen to no more lectures this day!

Crow flew upward two branches. He'd watch her from here.

Plum turned her attention to the white house at the top of the sloping yard. Now that she was so tiny, no more than two inches, human houses were quite monstrous to her, like the homes of giants. But this house fascinated her more than any of the others. She had flown over the town numerous times now, both in the sparkling sunlight and in the hazy moonlight, trying to espy something familiar, something that would spur her memory. She longed to know from where she came, who she truly was, and why she was now the most minuscule person. Perhaps the house was part of the answer. She was drawn to examine its warped windows, worn shingles, slanted porch. Something in there was good, because she sensed it. She felt sweetened and favored when she lingered near it. But something in there was *not* so good, too.

That sensation was like a warning, gave her a briefly fevered and uneasy heart.

So Plum watched the house while Crow watched Plum.

In mid-afternoon, a boy came into the backyard. He was about nine in human years, but rather small, and apparently quite sad. He was trying not to cry, but the effort was great and once he shuddered and gasped lightly, like a baby just being soothed.

What was this? Unhappiness? Pain? Plum was immediately vigilant, immediately ready to champion the small boy.

But before she flew to him, the boy, with one quick glance at the house, ran toward the end of the yard, and stopped on the other side of Plum's tree. There he sat down, leaning against the trunk. His head was bowed and his hands clutched his knees. Hiding? Praying? Those were most precious hands, brown-skinned, a little dirty, but somehow suggesting loneliness. Oh! Plum would hold those hands if she could. But being so tiny, she'd likely be held herself. Though she already felt richly fond of the child, she also felt wary.

CAW!

Plum lifted her gaze momentarily to Crow, who had stretched his wings up and out, making himself appear much larger and even threatening. He actually hissed! Plum shushed him with a piercing look and with a finger across her beautiful lips. She was indignant that Crow could be alarmed by a sobbing child.

"Mean creature," she whispered. "Bully. Brute."

Crow dropped from the higher branch to her own, and she heard his thought. "'Tis not Crow who's the brute!"

Plum spun around to see the house again. Now adults and children were coming into the backyard. Two men moved a long wooden table into the shade of the maple tree, and a woman spread a lovely blue cloth over the table.

Other humans brought platters and bowls of food, plates, glasses.

A feast! The humans were celebrating. Why, then, was this child hiding?

One woman had strolled down from the others and was obviously looking for the child. She was, yes, a pretty woman, though she seemed tired. "John!" she called. "John? Honey, we're getting ready to eat. Please come. Everyone wants to see you."

Below Plum, the boy responded by slipping and sliding down the incline, across the bit of water, and along the other narrow bank into shadows of larger, more overhanging limbs.

"You follow him," Plum directed Crow, and turned her own gaze back to the human woman, who gave one longing look toward the trees, tilted her head as though sighing, then walked dejectedly back to the others. Plum shut her eyes and willed herself into the maple tree above the humans, but it didn't work. When she opened them, she was in the same place as before, and with an amused Crow—though how a crow can look amused she could not explain—looking at her.

"And what are you doing here?" she said, with one light stamp of her foot. "Did I not tell you to follow the lad and care for him?"

Crow dropped down next to her, nudged her off the limb, then swooped beneath her and caught her deftly in the soft hollow between wing and back. "I can fly myself," she asserted toward the shiny black head. She sensed no reply and thought perhaps Crow was angry. He released her, a bit roughly, at a three-branch divide in the pecan tree, where she had ample pacing room. As Crow alighted on a lower branch, she heard inside, "Friends are asked, not ordered." Now she had a sad little boy and a huffy Crow!

Sitting above the humans, ever so comfortable in her

smooth perch, Plum at first could see no reason for the boy's unhappiness or anger. The people below seemed jolly enough. They laughed often. They also ate freely, and the food looked so very appetizing. Plum considered practicing magic. Could she bring herself a shrunken portion of the chicken? Now what would be the spell? But she heard a sound like CAW and HARRUMPH together and wondered if chicken and crow were too similar for her companion's comfort. She turned to find Crow not far behind her, trying to hide behind a cluster of leaves. She puckered her red-bow mouth and blew him a kiss—not a sincere kiss at all, a teasing kiss. Crow's head stayed in view, as if accepting the gesture.

She turned her attention to each human, adult and child. Why were they frightening to her now-favorite child? The woman who talked the most had a voice that boomed till Plum felt herself almost knocked from the tree. She had to tune down her senses so that voice and others became softer and intelligible.

"John is just wanting attention," the boomer declared, lavishing butter onto a wonderful-looking roll. "He knows it hurts you for him not to join us. If you would ignore him, he'd come around much sooner."

The listener—the woman who had walked down to call after the boy—shook her head, and red curls bounced. She wasn't a young woman, but she certainly was comely. There was gentleness, hope, and sadness in her face. "If he does it to hurt me," she said to the larger woman, "it's because he's hurting and doesn't know how to handle it. I can't make his father visit him."

"We're his family, too."

"But he doesn't *feel* like you are. You're my sisters. We're women. He wants his father."

"What about Argul? You two have remarried and he's

John's dad now. He doesn't mistreat the boy, does he?" The pretty woman didn't answer immediately, and Plum held her breath. She was afraid of the answer.

"No more than he mistreats the rest of us."

Plum wanted to be big, right now, to be a strong, and perhaps mean, witch. Why did she have to wake up in this very backyard and be so little, so next to nothing, that she couldn't even cast a proper spell? And who was this Argul, who made sweet people so very miserable? She would right this wrong, oh yes! This very day if she could. Crow suddenly alighted at her side, and she felt even more strengthened.

"We'll save the boy John and the mother, too," she said.

"There's a girl, older than the boy."

"We'll save her as well."

"All things come at a cost," she heard.

Plum looked up into one downcast beady eye. "I'll pay it," she said. "And gladly." With one longing look at the feast below, especially the few bits of chicken left on the huge platter, she lifted herself aloft and, to disguise herself, flew in the lazy side-to-side way of a bumblebee. She hummed, too, a high burr, in an imitation of the bee's sound.

"Some bird may eat you," she heard, as Crow went swooping by.

"Best not, since I ate no bird."

"Point taken."

Plum burred and buzzed through the trees draping over the rivulet, searching with her keen eyesight for the boy who willfully kept himself hidden from that loving and worried woman. No! She immediately corrected herself and lost a little height from the realization, almost colliding with an apple. The boy wasn't hiding from the *woman*, but from the unseen foe, the monster named Argul, who was mean to all and sundry. She quickened her search.

Moments later, she saw the boy. John. He was still in the creek bed, but under an embankment that curved outward, forming a wide shelter, like the mouth of a large cave. Roots of a thorn tree had broken through the soil above and dangled down, like misshapen fingers and arms. He was on his knees, bending over a flat stone. Plum lighted on a small honeysuckle bush growing almost perpendicularly above the boy (honeysuckles are brave and hardy plants). There she could see what John was doing, and her heart fluttered so much she almost fell from the bush. He was holding the prong of a forked stick against the wide, fat neck of a frog. The frog, thankfully on his stomach, so the prong wasn't pressing against his vulnerable soft throat, was still obviously in great distress. His eyes, which bulged naturally in the best of conditions, were now hideously distended and had also gone hazy and still. Immensely frightened, he had accepted death, preferring to go into shock and feel nothing rather than struggle. John, the wicked lad, though he didn't press harder with the stick, was whispering, "Die! Die! Die!"

A pained "Oh!" escaped Plum's lips and she needed to be able to stamp her foot to vent her own distress, which was mostly fear and anger. "Oh!" she said again, and two things happened at the sound. John looked in her direction as if he had actually heard her. And Crow appeared, landing on the damp soil a few feet to the side of John, but not quite in the water.

John had returned his attention to the frog. He carefully turned it over and pressed the prong against that velvety throat that can swell and throb with sound. How to stop him? How to stop him? Now John was holding the stick with his left hand and searching for something in his pocket. He brought forth a small knife! He opened it with his teeth!

She must act. With no plans whatsoever, Plum zoomed pell-mell into John's lifted hand. The knife fell, but so did

Plum, right onto the limestone next to the frog. Though a little dazed, she saw that one side of the prong was raised, and the frog could slip out if he'd move. Though lying on her back, and still dizzy, she booted the frog's rounded side. "Get up," she said, booting him again. "Get up and save yourself, you foolish quivering thing."

He couldn't have escaped, of course, except that John was himself apparently in shock, his brown eyes so locked on Plum that she might have felt hypnotized if she had looked at them too long. The frog was plop, inches away, plop, a foot away, plop, plop, plop, plop, in the water, swissssssssshhhhh-hhhhh, under water yards away, only his eyes above the surface. They appeared slightly crossed now. He was a smarter frog.

Meanwhile, Plum had stood up and raised one fist, while the other hand was on her waist, as if she were scolding a child of her own, one much smaller than she was. "You are not a good child," she yelled upward. "Most certainly not! You are an unkind boy. An evil boy! Yes. Evil. And Plum was worried about you? You *should* hide from other human beings. You don't deserve..."

"CAW!"

She continued her sentence but couldn't hear the words because Crow was CAWING loudly and stridently, and also hopping toward her and the boy. Well, she wasn't through with John, no she wasn't, and Crow couldn't—

John had her in his hand. It closed around her so tightly there was no light at all, and it was hot and wet and gritty from dirt and her cheek hurt. Then, suddenly, a loud, sharp cry like the sky tore open, then sunlight and she fell, only to be batted upward by one silk wing, then upward again, then tossed onto the wide, safe back of Crow.

When her breath became even, when the sun stopped streaming so brightly that she could recognize the land below, the houses, the creek bed, she said, "I could've saved myself. I wasn't ready."

In her head she heard, "You're not ready in many ways, my beloved."

"What's that?" she demanded of Crow, but he flew steadily forward. "What was the last thing you said?" Moments later, she had zoomed ahead and to one side, so she could watch Crow's face as she questioned him. "What was it? You tell me, Crow! Did you say 'beloved'? Crows can't love people! Crow?" He didn't respond at all, simply flew back to the tree they had made their home. She followed and landed next to him.

"Well?"

He remained silent, crouched in his normal resting spot.

She flounced away, into her rooms. She went about cleansing herself, occasionally coming to the hollow opening to observe Crow and to listen to the pleasant, rumbling and clattering sounds of humans. The sunlight weakened, turned a faint gold, then a dusky rose, as the sun set. Dressed only in pantaloons, Plum looked out at the brooding Crow. "'Beloved'?" she thought to herself.

Seconds later she distinctly heard inside, "'Tis difficult to love arrogance."

Her back went rigid. Her small face flushed. "Arrogant?" she said aloud. "Arrogant? Who's arrogant?"

She heard the rustle of his movements, then saw his dark form ascending. "Crow," she called. "Crow."

For a while, sitting in the center of her petal bed, she tried to conjure up clothing, a nightgown, a boy's attire, a plainer, lighter dress, a camisole. Anything. She tried closing her eyes, speaking the name of the item, singing it, waving her hands. Nothing. The room grew dimmer. She wearied.

She was alone and with no skills, no art. And maybe she had an enemy. Could a human boy find her? What powers *did* she have? Could she even save herself? She hadn't done too well so far.

She lay back, her eyes troubled and sad. "Crow?" she thought. "I'm afraid to be alone." Just as she turned onto her side so she could watch the doorway, she heard a soft whooshing outside, and a responding voice inside. "You're not alone."

So she slept.

In the morning, her purple gown was still on its briar hook, but the cloth now gleamed clean and fresh, as if newly made. And behind it shone a tinge of white. Plum left her bed to investigate, though she suspected what she would find. A nightdress, delicate and new, with lace across the bodice.

She didn't understand. "I still need new pantaloons," she said aloud to whomever or whatever, or to herself if she was doing this without knowing it. "And a set of pants would be much appreciated. It is difficult to move in heavy silk, much less move quickly." She heard the discontent in her own voice, and, after a moment of silence while she controlled herself, she muttered, "One thanks you."

"It's a new day," she heard. Crow was awake.

"You needn't tell me!" she asserted. "I was working even in my sleep."

THE CATCH

*P*lum could not find an entry to the house. "I'm a fairly poor witch," she muttered, "if I can't enter a building so big as this." She was most irritated, but also most pleased that the family took such good care of their home. Though very old, the house was neatly tight—cracks sealed, windows and screens flush with the jambs, attic vents covered with fine mesh. No unwanted insect or creature would find easy access. Perhaps the mister here wasn't all mean spirit. "Oh, if I could just blink myself in there." But just thinking didn't work, no matter how she scrunched closed her eyes. Apparently, witch skills did not come automatically, and she had forgotten hers, along with other knowledge—such as who she was, where she came from, and why she was only two inches tall! That, more than anything, she would like to remember. But now—to get inside this house.

With a deep breath, she flew to the front porch behind Crow, who landed quite capably on the wooden floor. Plum chose the back of the porch swing. "Are you going to knock?" she asked, delighted with her own humor.

She knew he responded, "Perhaps," though he did not look toward her. In the ludicrous manner of crows, he walked toward the door and, just before reaching it, flew suddenly upward, pecked a round metal button, and landed again with awkward dignity. High-pitched, clear bells chimed. "What is that tune?" Plum said. "I know it!"

"Doorbell," Crow said hurriedly. "Get ready." He flew up to the porch eave, out of sight, and Plum, in panic, zoomed up, hovering near the porch-light globe. The main door opened, the screen door swung out only inches, and in that brief moment Plum looped in and up, landing in the first convenient place, which turned out to be the pleated top of heavy, long curtains dividing two rooms. With her lips parted, and her breathing still too quick, Plum watched the pretty mother close the door and peer around the living room ceiling as if she had heard something. Plum crunched down into a pleat fold, her eyes shut, and hoped the search did not continue.

When the footsteps moved away, Plum stayed hidden a hard moment more, then raised up and gazed around this human dwelling. It was humble, yes. But warm and neat. She maneuvered herself between the panels of the green curtain and surveyed the adjoining room. A bedroom with an old four-poster bed, a dresser with two silk-shaded lamps, a broad and deep-blue chair, not velvet, but similar, and patterned in etched roses. The wallpaper depicted tiny women, each with a parasol, approaching narrow, wooden, arched bridges. Above the bed on one side was a small, framed picture. Before Plum could investigate more, she heard lighter steps in the front room, and she returned, pulling herself back up to the rod and pleats.

"Whew," Plum sighed. "Thank goodness I am somewhat strong." She settled down to watch her human boy.

In moments, despite John's earlier behavior toward the

frog, she adored him. He had a sweet-urchin quality, like a good-natured, kind, gentle spirit that was now bedraggled from too much worry. He was tiny-boned, slender, but with the roundness of extreme youth still softening all his features. The smooth light tan of his skin turned rosy on his cheekbones, forearms, and hands. Nothing in the soft brown eyes now suggested cruelty. Perhaps he had never hurt anything, and she had thwarted his first attempt. She hoped that was true. Oh! Those reddish lips should be smiling. Plum was going to see that they did. But how?

Again, someone was approaching from the kitchen. The person stepped from the shadows into the sun-filled living room. A handsome man. A truly handsome man. Rangy, with unusually fair skin, a wide full mouth, and startlingly clear, pleasant blue eyes. Well, this was a most beautiful family, was it not? Was this the father? Was this the monster Argul? That could not be.

"Hey, John," the man said. "Did you know I was home?"

A very, very small nod indicated yes.

"How you been? Your mom says you've taken up fishing?"

Another nod. Why would John not speak?

"Maybe we could go together sometime?"

This time John's lips shaped "maybe," though Plum heard nothing. So! The monster was fond of the urchin. But the urchin? He wanted nothing to do with the friendly, blue-eyed ... Monster? Man. Yes. Nothing to do with the friendly, blue-eyed, and handsome man.

When, moments later, the man opened the front door, Plum slipped out just behind and above him. There, she landed on the back of the swing, immensely grateful for the fresh air, for the prospects of a day following the little human, and a day in the company of Crow, who was perhaps her servant. Yes. Witches had servants.

"I serve where I will," she heard. "But I am no servant."

"I'm just trying to understand who I am and what has happened to me."

"Then concern yourself with your own nature and leave mine to me."

"Done, sir! You needn't be so stern with your friends."

"Nor you so possessive with yours."

Silence while they both brooded a little bit and waited on the boy to guide them to fishing.

"These humans," Plum heard Crow think, "are not all that handsome."

"Surely they are."

"Because you're fond of them. They come lovelier."

"Not to me."

"You can be loyal. That's not a bad trait."

"I have no bad traits," Plum asserted.

"Shame."

Plum agreed. She flew to a rose bush and sat in the center of a white blossom. A cat was creeping toward a tree, and Plum planned to dive at him before he could hurt any bird in her yard, and especially in Crow's presence. She broke off a tiny, tiny thorn, which would serve as a lovely, curved knife to surprise a mean, sneaky cat. But she needn't have worried. A blue jay tweaked the cat's tail and terrified Plum back to the porch and Crow's umbrella of safety.

Plum followed John, and she enjoyed the traveling. The countryside reminded her of stories she couldn't quite remember. The sun glowed butterscotch rich and the land below was many shades and textures of life, like a giant quilt of summer. Trees curled and branched thickly not far from the road, on both sides, and beyond them lay stretches of tended land, planted with corn and soybeans. From her higher vantage point, Plum saw the careful rowing of orchards, where trees were encouraged to grow a healthy distance from one another, saw the pitch of roofs on red barns, white barns, saw spirals of dust raised by men on tractors, clothes drying on lines, swallows on power lines, saw a hawk.

A hawk? Hawk!

"Crow!" she called and glanced up so quickly that she lost control momentarily and zoomed a few perilous yards downward. Clenching her eyes and thinking UP, UP, UP, she felt the downward trajectory ease and felt herself rising. She opened one eye. Yes, the magic had worked this time.

Now, where was Crow?

Looking more carefully, Plum saw him sailing in an angle down, away from the hawk. The latter, a ravenous creature and a formidable hunter, was in the attack position, talons jutting and grasping, wings arched for swoop.

Oh! Plum gasped, but she couldn't scream. She dare not divert Crow's attention even one second. He plummeted directly in the hawk's path, which was intended to intercept his own. Then, just as Crow neared the safety of tangled green leaves, Crow disappeared. Now, was that true? Plum asked herself, shaking her wee head and standing still in midair, an ability she hadn't known she had. Crow disappeared? Poof?

The hawk, on the upward swing of the failed attack, also seemed perplexed. He retraced his descent and on the second rising, seemed to recall Plum.

"Oh no, you don't," she muttered, and let herself drop, planning to fly near John whose presence would surely ward off danger. And it did ward off the danger presented by the hawk; but it offered another kind. No sooner was Plum positioned a few yards behind the lad, than he turned so quickly she hadn't time to avoid his direct gaze. He saw her fully, most surely, most certainly he did. Walking backwards, he studied her with those sad eyes, not appearing amused or enthralled or enchanted. He held the fishing rod over his shoulder, and from its tip dangled a silver hook.

Plum shivered. Would he hurt her? Was he capable of such cruelty? She couldn't tell, though his eyes were distant, pained. She felt much like apologizing—for what, she didn't know.

He turned again, walking on. And suddenly Crow appeared, coming from the trees, nearing them, and finally floating above, in restrained zigzags.

She sent a thought toward Crow. "Where did you go?"

"Just down," came his silent answer.

"Down? You disappeared. You best remember I was watching."

"And I watched even closer. It was my experience, if you will. I folded my wings and dropped dead. It was a fast fall, with wings tucked." He dipped his right wing. "And a planned fall," he added.

"You played dead! You played possum. Such a sly Crow!"

Came the indignant reply, "Crafty, not sly. Crafty. Friends must choose words carefully."

"Craft. Oh yes."

"And I played crow, not possum. Possums have their place, and are good creatures overall, but grace is not one of their traits. Not that they're to blame."

"I understand, Crow. You may leave possums out of our conversation."

"They're good foragers. And mothers. They make . . ."

"Crow! Enough!"

"I wouldn't want to injure any creature," Crow said, "by not conceding to their value."

"Possums are wonderful, wonderful, wonderful," Plum said shrilly, not one of her endearing tones, and Crow flew a bit higher.

Plum felt corrected, which wasn't pleasant. But her irritation vanished. Crow's shadow passed over her, like a touch of steady, strong spirit. She was learning to trust him. He was a fine but mysterious creature, that Crow.

JOHN'S FISHING place suited him—private, almost hidden, with no trace of travel to and from the pool. He often approached by a different direction, so the forest growth was undisturbed. Vines interlaced, branches pressed heavily against one another, and sometimes layered, like ladders formed by a merging of trees. The ground was moist from the nearby river, from underground water, and from the natural cycling of life.

Plum had found herself a good vantage point, atop a mossy boulder covered with cracks and holes, all of them a possible home or rest area for small creatures. Crow joined her.

John had finished play-casting. Now he was on knees, quickly removing items from his backpack. A tiny iron skillet. Why would he carry such a thing? He extracted also containers of some kind Plum couldn't recognize. He spread them on a ragged gray towel brought, it seemed, for just that purpose. Then, standing, he strode purposefully toward the woods again, into the growth, and reemerged moments later with an armful of small branches, obviously stored there from an earlier visit. A few feet from the water's edge, he lowered the wood into a neat pile, knelt and began scooping loose dirt as if to bury something. But to Plum's surprise, he uncovered a stone-lined circle. Oh, he was clever! He had covered traces of his former fires, yet kept the site prepared for his return.

With the fire started, John removed another container and peeled back the lid.

Plum squinched shut her eyes. She knew. Worms. She

shuddered. Worms. When she looked again, the line was sailing over the water, sinking into it, leaving a yellow ball bobbing on the surface. She thought of what hung beneath. "Worms. Ugh!"

"I eat them," she heard.

"Surely not!"

"Sometimes worse things."

"Oh Crow. I'll fetch food for you."

"I said I eat them. 'Tis not a matter of desire or preference. 'Tis, unfortunately, my nature."

Plum understood, though she wasn't sure how.

"I'm truly sorry," she said, which obviously was the correct answer, because Crow tilted his head down, looking a little puzzled, but also pleased.

A quick movement from the shore caught Plum's attention. John had been successful. Though he had made no vocal sound, not even a gasp of pleasure or victory, all his movements showed mastery and happiness. The pole was bent from the struggle of the hooked creature, but the fisherman was well experienced. Though how? So young? He reeled smoothly, keeping the tip of the rod up and the line tight. Near shore, the fish cleared the water, shone a gray silver, and splashed back. John drew it to shore, carried it by line safely back from the water, and only then, kneeling, did he survey his catch. He seemed very proud. He raised his eyes and scanned the area, as if looking for another living creature. His gaze stopped at Plum's hiding place, and she was certain he knew she was present, even if he couldn't see her. But perhaps he could! Who knew what human children could do. Or would do. He returned his attention to the fish. He spoke to it, and then firmly and quickly gripping it close behind its wide head, he simultaneously pressed down the fins and held it still, while his right hand deftly removed the hook. He stood, carried the tail-thrashing, handsome fish to the water's edge and tossed it back. Threw it back!

Crow's beak was open. Plum was zipping out over the water, mindless of who or what might see her, trying to see if the fish were really alive. And there it was. A quick curve of silver, again, again, and gone. Well. Plum hovered one moment more and saw another, fatter form approach the surface, arching up, and buzzzzztt, Plum got back to her rock.

"Bass," thought Crow. "Thought you were a fly, most likely."

"A fly?"

"Haw!" not an ugly sound, meant as a laugh, she knew.

Now the boy fisherman knelt by his fire, putting a small bit of lard into the skillet, placing the skillet over the steady flame, and then dropping a slice of bread into the pan. After a brief time, he flipped the bread with his as-yet-unused knife. When he removed the skillet to a flat rock, he knifed the bread into his hand, then slipped it back and forth between both hands till it had cooled. Sitting cross-legged by the water, facing its glittering expanse, he ate the bread.

Plum was so charmed by him, so enchanted at his generous gesture of freeing the fish, that she only slowly realized that a repeated whistle from the woods sounded not like a bird at all, but like a human pretending to be something he wasn't. Plum was up, on her feet, suddenly feeling encumbered by the heavy skirt of her gown. She wished it off! She wished it gone! Gone!

But there it stayed. Why did her wishing work for one thing and not another? Such whimsical powers were almost useless.

A group of boys slightly older than her charge emerged from the woods. There were six of them, and all bigger than John.

Plum readied herself. She must be rid of the heavy skirt. On the right side of Plum's gown was a lady's pocket, just a shallow pouch capable of holding a folded silk handkerchief. Now she grabbed one side of the pocket with each hand and tugged with all her might. A corner ripped. She tugged again, ripping the cloth around her torso.

The band was headed straight for her human, who had kicked dirt over his fire and quickly stuffed his containers into his backpack. Only the skillet, still cooling, and the rod were still in the open. And John.

Plum quickly tore the skirt from the waist down till she could step free of it, now dressed in a purple top and white pantaloons.

The lanky boy who had led the group forward spoke to the young fisherman. "I knew you were sneaking onto somebody's land."

"I didn't sneak."

"Oh, yes you did. We watched. You were hiding all the time."

John shook his head. "Nope. I walked right down the highway." He had a soft, mellow voice, soothing, even if he were afraid.

"I mean after you turned into the woods," said the challenger. "You didn't want anybody to see where you went."

"It's a good fishing hole."

"It's not yours."

That was the crux, apparently, for all of them. The five friends of the speaker stood in a semicircle behind him, all their eyes turned to the fisher boy.

"No," John assented, bending to pick up the skillet, "it's not. But it's not yours, either." He slipped the pan into his pack, fastened the flap, and turned to take up his rod. Just before his hand touched the delicate wood, his attacker darted forward, snatched the rod by the slender tip, and broke it across his knee.

John, Plum's only concern, looked stricken. His lips were parted, his eyes bright with shock and pain, and his cheeks an angry red.

"Do nothing!" she whispered, though had she shouted he probably would have been unable to hear. "Just let them finish. Let them go."

"Sissy fella," the bully said. "We saw you throw the fish back. Couldn't even kill it. Eat it proper. Ate bread instead."

Those words caused John, who had still been staring at his destroyed rod, to raise his head. "I'm not a sissy," he said, his voice steady. "I could skin you."

A rustling sounded from the group, as if they would run or attack. The bully licked his lips.

But right at that moment, the boy turned his back to them, as if they were dismissed. Plum held her breath. Such daring and fortitude for a child. He took his pack, faced them again, and strode forward as if nothing were in his path. The semicircle of young men parted for him, and his attacker, now with half a rod in each hand and the line dangling between them, just turned to watch. Then, as if realizing he had to say something to remain in authority, he called, "Don't come back here. Next time I'll break you instead of your rod."

With those words, he tossed the broken rod away as if it hurt his hands.

Plum, acting without thinking, as had always been her wont to do, and unhampered by a heavy gown, zipped like a dart, bit the bully on the earlobe three times, pinching, too, then zipped up and away. A cry of more than one voice sounded behind her, but she didn't turn back. She swooped down, beside her brown-berry boy, where of course he could see her if he but looked up. He didn't. He strode on, head down, steadily, firmly, and oh! now she could see why. Was he crying, then? Really? Her own heart was breaking at the silence and pride of his pain.

She stayed his companion the long trek to the paved road, and then down and up its forever-taking path to his home.

At some point, Crow joined them, making his presence known by a concerned voice inside Plum's head. "That's a sorry lot of humans back there. Thank Heavens they're young enough to change."

"Don't worry about them!" Plum thought in reply. "Don't mention them in the same breath with John."

"I didn't. You just did." Crow flapped away raggedly, as if he were weary of her.

Crow was haughty! But he was right. She flew low and by John till he opened the screen door of his mother's house. Then she followed him but stayed close to the seam of ceiling and wall. Now his head was up, and he even seemed wary, though this was his own home and the bullies far away. Halfway down the hall, at the entrance to his room, he slipped free of the backpack and set it just inside his door. He went on to the kitchen. Plum followed.

His mother was alone at the sink, humming a lovely tune. Atop the stove, dinner cooked—a browned beef roast sizzling in its own juices, potatoes boiling rivulets of broth over the edge of a pan, yellow corn with bubbling butter and pepper. Plum wanted never to eat just berries and nuts again. She was a hearty two inches of life. She needed real food.

Her care returned immediately to John, who was now moving toward his mother. She sensed or heard him, and turned, drying her hands by flattening them against her white apron.

"John? Honey?" She held out her arms and he stepped into them, his head reaching only a little above her waist. "Honey? Baby what's wrong?" She started to kneel down, but he pulled away as if controlling himself. Plum saw the shudder of his body, like a chill through him, and knew control took all his remaining strength.

"They broke my fishing pole," he said, in a gentle and wavering voice.

"Who? Who did that?"

"Phil McGhee."

"Why?"

He shrugged. His mother's hand guided him against her once more, while she looked out the window as if the monster that would devour him stood there and would have to devour her first. "I don't know, John, why people have to do such cruel things." Her hand cupped the back of his head.

"It was the only thing I had," he said, and Plum saw the mother's reaction in her eyes, and heard a reaction behind her, too, a quick gasp. His sister, now hurrying up the hall with her hands pressed over her mouth as if to quieten herself.

Plum had to escape. No one could look long on despair. She flew to the living room, preparing to bide her time in the heavy curtain, but she didn't have to. The freckled sister jerked the front door open for her own exit and Plum glided out. The girl was crying and Plum thought the whole world would likely dissolve in tears if she didn't do something to right everything immediately. But she had no strength either. Sadness was a powerful thing. It ate all hope very fast.

In the sweet heartsick of late afternoon, Plum floated back to her tree, to her safe, guarded, hollow home. She began looking for Crow even before she landed, and then afterward, and finally saw his form many branches up. He was somewhat hunched, as if sleeping.

"Crow," she said.

He didn't answer.

"Crow. Don't be cross with me. We have to care for one another, you know. No one else will."

"It's about time you're thinking of that," he thought toward her, accompanying it with three hoarse caws.

"Will you come down then?"

"Maybe not."

Oh, he was a worrisome male. "Then I'll come up."

"'Twould be best."

In one swift ascent, she was alighting next to him on the narrow limb. "Why here, where you have to cling so?" she asked.

"I need to cling at the moment, missy. I need to fasten my claws in a tight circle, so I won't fall off."

The leaves were shimmering myriad shades of green behind and above him, as if the sunlight were green and reflecting on water. His eyes were fierce, fiery, wanting. Perhaps that's what drew her attention closer, down, and she saw the wet patch of soft feathers at the joint of wing and body. Blood! He was injured. Oh, shame to her.

"Crow!" she cried, placing her hand ever so gently against that same wing. "I didn't know. I wouldn't have left you to fly alone."

She heard his voice inside, pained and reserved. "I encountered a thrown stone or two after you followed the boy and then I found you and left on my own. You are not responsible."

Plum sat down as close as she could beside him. His black claws gripped the limb tightly. Not once would she leave him tonight, nor would she sleep. This night she was Crow's guardian. He would not fall; she would see to that. If he did, she would bear him back up with her own body.

In the night, Plum awoke. Crow was now on her other side, and his good wing was held out just enough to cloak her. On the rise beyond, the kitchen window of John's house glowed. Someone was still awake there. Perhaps all of them. She bowed her head. Truly, she did not have the strength to know more right now. And if someone needed her, that someone was Crow. Already she had let him down, by sleeping—for the rest of the night, she would be vigilant. Vigilant. Feathers around her ruffled, as if a night breeze stirred them.

"Just rest," she heard. "'Tis difficult to care for all at once, and lessons come hard."

Lessons? Was she in training then? "Who are you, Crow?" she demanded, forgetting for a moment that he, too, must rest.

The weariness in his voice shamed her for her impatience. "I am Crow and that is enough for me. Perhaps I will be more than Crow later. But such thoughts are too much for a simple mind that needs peace." A rapid, fine shiver went through his feathers, as if he stretched and settled them for the night. His head tucked a little more, and the voice came again, even softer, like he sighed himself into sleep. "Perhaps you should worry about who is Plum."

Plum lay her head against him, his feathers like black silk beneath her cheek. But who could sleep when such a riddle had been dropped before her? The moon was high up, a tantalizing light shone from the house, and Plum? She was hungry, she was. And sitting in her pantaloons and half a dress beside a superior, infuriating, self-righteous, and quite dear Crow. She felt him smiling even in his dream.

A LITTLE MISS WITH THE DEVIL

rue to her best intentions, Plum stayed by Crow as he healed, except for brief trips to get necessary supplies. She found a plant much like aloe, and pierced a leaf to gather its healing gel on a petal, which she applied to his wound. She gathered their food and water, stood guard, tried to be totally subservient to her friend's needs. She did well, but her mind *would* follow tangents. "Have you ever wondered what colors we do not see?" she asked half-dozing Crow. "Suppose we woke and our eyes saw only the newest hues? Suppose grass had become the color of raspberries?"

Inside her head, where she always heard Crow's responses—and in her own voice, too—she heard, "Do you want an answer? Or do you want to pour questions for a while?"

"Both," she asserted, glad that he was a bit snippy, which indicated a healthy Crow, and irritated that he often seemed to feel superior to her. That, of course, was not possible. Not possible at all. "First," she said, "answer what you will and then I will question what I want."

"I have never wondered what colors I do not see. I am satisfied that I see at all."

"Oh, you wicked, high-minded Crow. I feel the same. Everyone is most grateful for blessings."

He was now quiet, which Plum had not intended. "Go on," she said.

"Are you certain? I would like to finish a thought."

Now Plum held her silence, though it was not comfortable, and in moments Crow's thoughts continued. "How do you know that we see the same colors now? And if *we* do," he looked down into the yard as if scanning for other creatures, "how do you know that others see the same? Someone," he added in a somber, almost wary, tone, "may *already* see raspberry grass."

Plum gasped and immediately confirmed that the grass below was still green, the sky blue, the house white, that the world had not again transformed while she was unaware, as it had done when she woke to find herself so tiny. "That is a most wonderful answer," she said. "You truly have a fine mind, Crow. You make the world more miraculous than it already is." Now she was the subdued one, peering off as if her vision had been changed. In a moment, though, she stood up, holding onto a slightly untucked feather on Crow's healthy wing, and stretched her wee self while yawning widely. Crow, watching with one eye, admired the unusual pose. While he understood that she was an adult, human movements in such small degree were utterly charming.

"Well," she said. "What will you dine on tonight?"

"I feel well enough to find my own food."

"And you may do so starting tomorrow," she said. "How about corn?"

"When did you become enamored of corn? Never have I eaten so much—"

She was gone. Crow watched the high line of her flight

till he could see her no more, and for one brief moment experienced a deep pain at that possibility. He must see her again. Every day of his life. He dropped his head, as if sleeping. What woe! Perhaps this fondness would pass, like an illness or immaturity. Behind his closed eyes, though, he could image her sweet face in all its lovely detail. He had known it for so long. She returned many times, leaving another morsel or two, seeds, an unblemished strawberry, a minute tomato. Below and behind Crow, the yard and ditch teemed with the kind of food he now ate. In one swoop, he could find more nourishment than Plum would bring him in an entire evening. He was hungry, and if he continued to eat only what Plum provided, he would starve to death. Truly.

THEN IT WAS a weekend morning again, though Plum had no real sense of days of the week and saw the pattern only in human lives she observed. The morning was a late summer one, when the air, though warm, somehow conveyed that fall was nearing, days shortening. Plum, at an open window in hopes of seeing John, was instead seeing his sister, about eleven, who sang a sad tune as she cleaned the kitchen. Plum much enjoyed the voice—clear, and sweet, yet strong, especially for a child. Plum might be only two inches tall, but she was a young adult, certainly more mature than the singing child, and very sympathetic with the unhappiness she sensed in the girl. Was the whole family, then, unhappy? What was Plum to do?

The girl put aside her cleaning tools, came to the window apparently to make sure the mother was still in the backyard, hanging clothes. Then the girl turned on a stove burner and, to Plum's consternation, passed her forearm through the flame, and then did it again. Plum zoomed to the clothesline, hovering behind the mother's head and thus out of her sight, but making such a racket the woman was sure to think herself under attack by a bumblebee. In seconds, the woman hurried toward the house, still bent over, hand capping her head. Plum darted first to the kitchen window, through which she saw the girl now passing her other arm through the fire. Aghast at such behavior, Plum hung in plain view while the mother entered the kitchen, startled at her daughter's action, snapped off the burner, and ushered the girl to the sink where she ran water over her daughter's forearms. Suddenly the woman was at the window, fanning the air outward, and Plum dropped down rapidly, landing in a small red wagon the woman often used to haul small loads. "You could have caught on fire, Catherine! You could've burned the house down! What if I were sleeping or at the store? Girl, girl, what am I going to do with you? It is natural to have hair on your arms, and on your legs. And natural to have freckles. And some girls, Catherine, would love to have curly hair. Why can't you accept yourself?"

"I'm ugly."

"You are not ugly! Far from it. But you will be, if you keep acting like this. Something will go wrong and you may not be the only person who suffers."

"It didn't work anyway. The hair on my arm is singed close, and brown, and smells bad."

"Don't let me hear any more about this," the woman said. "Think about what you have. Some people would be thankful even to have arms."

Oh! Why frighten the child? Why make her feel guilt? Plum wanted to go in the house, soothe that human girl, and assure her that she was quite lovely and would become more so. Plum was certain of this. And even if it weren't true, the child deserved hope and encouragement, not threat. The mother could help her daughter remove the remaining, scorched hair. Cool the skin, lotion it. Sympathize. Until now, Plum had liked the mother. Horrid woman!

Just at that thought, at that very moment, when Plum was poised to lift up to the window, something dropped around her, something clear, and heavy, and hard. Glass! Through it she could see a human hand closing round, and beyond, glimpses of a human face, ruddy skin. The tormentor from the fishing hole. Something slid beneath her, making her lose her footing, and then she was unable to stand. She was being lifted, with cardboard beneath her, glass around her. Then the glass was upended, the cardboard on top and she on the bottom. She was in a wide jar! The glass distorted the light and the surroundings, so all Plum saw was moving color, streams and streaks of it. She was bouncing, getting quite bruised actually, but still so stunned that she wasn't afraid. In a short time, the colors ceased and shadows engulfed her. Movement slowed. The glass was still, placed on something solid. Light suddenly fanned up, high and wide, then settled. A candle, Plum surmised. Yes, she recognized the long, tapering tower. Once she had been large enough to hold such a candle, and have it be fairly narrow to her hands. No more. Something was rattling the glass, striking the cardboard ceiling, something very sharp! But it stopped. Her captor had been making air holes for her. Now she was under scrutiny, and so was he.

"I knew what I saw," he said, and the voice was like thunder until Plum allowed herself to hear only the finest tone of it. "And now I can prove it. If, that is, I can keep you alive."

"And what will you do with me?" she said. "Keep me in a jar?"

He had moved closer, squinting a little. "Are you talking? Is that you squeaking?" Up went the jar again. "What? What?"

His eyes were on her level, she could see her own silhouette in them, twin shadows of herself. It was quite disconcerting.

"Let me go," she said, only thinking it more than speaking, hoping that he could hear her thoughts as she could hear Crow's. "I have work to do. I have a friend to care for."

"What?"

Plum ceased talking. The candle was like a farm's vapor light, too glaring, unreal. And beyond it shadows, shapeless at first.

The cardboard lid moved and chips of something scattered down, at first frightening her. But he was taking care to drop them along the edge of the glass. Orangish, dry. Salt flecks like crystals. Crackers. He was feeding her cheese crackers. Well, let him. She wasn't going to eat. She sat quietly, face buried against her knees, refusing to let her concern be his entertainment. Occasionally his voice rumbled around her, but she didn't respond. Then she became aware of a heavier silence, no feeling of light, and she raised up. He was gone, and with him the candle. Instinctively, she flew up at the lid, hoping to dislodge it just by her momentum, but something weighted it down and stopped her so solidly she fell. Recovering, she tried flying from side to side of the glass, hoping to knock it over. Her weight was too slight. When she tired, and sat again, she had to fight twinges of fear, because how would anyone find her? She had only Crow to care, anyhow. She had no choice but to hope the boy, the tormentor, returned. After a span of time, perhaps hours, she broke off a handful of cracker, slipped a crumb into her mouth, then another. Moments later she regretted satisfying her hunger, because there was nothing here to satisfy her thirst.

"Crow," she thought. "Oh Crow."

She couldn't know that she was under a house, and that Crow, beside himself with his worry and his anger over having no powers, no powers at all, was stalking back and forth by the entry to the crawlspace. The boy had replaced the heavy cover and Crow could find no crack in the foundation large enough for himself. One crawlspace window had a corner broken out, but the hole was too small; if he forced his way inside, the glass might loosen and injure him more. Then who would help his wee human? His Plum? His worrisome, heartbreaking Plum.

The moon broke full above him, emerging from a cloud and making the night seem suddenly illuminated just for Crow, at his need, and with it came an idea. A tool! He needed something to crack the glass for him, and then he could enter and find his tiny companion. Off he went, on foot to spare his still mending wing, scurrying in that odd fashion of crows. Returning with a forked twig, he was unable to maneuver the wide part to put pressure against the pane. He heard something coming from the other side of the window, rustling. He neared, turning his head sideways to catch the sound. Something running, stopping, running again. "Plum!" he thought, hoping to sense her reply. Nothing came, but again the rustling. What could it be? He knew! Rats. A rat was after his human. Without thought for noise or for harming himself, Crow pecked the glass first inches away from the small hole, but each time closer and closer to the puncture and its jagged edges. The weakened glass broke suddenly beneath the pressure, and Crow's beak slipped through to the flesh. He pulled back painfully and pecked again. Shards of glass fell. He could now enter, and did so, clumsily, hurriedly, falling toward the earthen floor and spreading his wings just enough to ease the landing. "Plum!" he thought, but from his mouth issued the sharp "CAW!" that was his own sound. A second "CAW," followed by softer grunts. "Plum. Plum." He stumbled and staggered forward. To an outside viewer, he might have appeared drunken, and so he was—not with liquor, but with love and concern for another. He moved toward the direction of the rustling, hoping to encounter the maker before it encountered Plum, wherever she was.

Then he heard a familiar sound, high and sweet like a strain of music in his mind, and he took awkward bounding leaps for the last few feet, coming upon a glass jar with a piece of cardboard taped to the top, and just beyond the jar, a rat, huge, gray, with teeth bared and shiny, asserting owner-ship of the glass and its contents. Not so! Not to Crow! Another leap, another, the last with claws before him, so that, though he landed on his side and rolled to his back, his claws had the mighty rat—not for long, because it was a fierce creature, powerful and would have killed him, would have sunken those razor incisors into Crow's throat except that light exploded above the jar and horizontally, illuminating the underpinnings of the house, rusty cans, piles of rags, and, in far corners, beady eyes now waiting. Then Crow was up, seeing the light's source—a beam coming from the crawl-space. The boy!

"Crow! Here!" he heard, and turned toward the glass and its precious contents. He stumble-hopped his full weight against the glass and it fell sideways. He pecked rapidly at the tape, caught a bit of its edge with his beak, and peeled the tape and cardboard. Plum crawled out, buried her face and both hands in his thick feathers. "Help me, Crow," she said. "Get us out of here." He turned, headed for the darker recesses, away from the approaching light. His was a bounc-ing, loping run, the best he could do.

"Hey!" they both heard. "Hey! I brought you water. I'm not going to hurt you."

Neither of them believed the boy. They wanted the fresh air of outside and hope, not this dreadful burial at the mercy of others. They wanted freedom. Along the edge of the underhouse Crow ran, past the broken window and shards of glass, heading for the oblong paleness that was the crawl-space with its cover gone, like an opening into the heavens. Though he and Plum both heard something else moving, and knew it must be the boy, they didn't stop or even look, just kept their eyes and their direction toward the opening. Then they were beneath it and had only to fly or to maneuver themselves up the steps—steps they would have to attain by high leaps. Could they?

"Don't!" they heard. "Don't leave. Not now. Just let me give you the water. That's why I came back. I had to wait to sneak out. Didn't I feed you? Did I try to hurt you? Please. Wait."

"Should we?" Plum thought toward Crow. "He's telling the truth."

"No, we shouldn't." Crow's thought returned quickly and unmistakably firm. "He can give us water outside as well as inside. And what would he say had the rats come earlier? I'll take my water on solid ground, if you please."

But it wasn't to be, because Crow, try as he would, could not reach the highest step in time, and could not safely fly with Plum clutching his wing as she had been doing. The wing was almost as strong as before, but he might falter. Both wings—his entire body—were now filthy from running heedlessly through the underhouse and skir-mishing with a rat. The boy's hand, grabbing Crow roughly against the stone step, closed tightly enough to be uncom-fortable, but not to inflict real injury. Nonetheless, Crow delivered one half-force peck, and scratched with his claws. Then he fell still because struggling could harm his compan-ion, who was already half-submerged in the down of his underwing. They were caught, being jostled together crudely, with no discernible up or down for moments. Then they were aware of cooler, fresher air around the boy's hand. And a lighter darkness. Stars in the vast distance above.

"I'll let you go," they heard, a whisper loud to them, like a strong wind through thick leaves. "But let me look at you, okay? I want you to stay still." He had slowed and was apparently seated. His face, near them again, seemed not threatening.

"If he opens his hand," Crow directed silently, "flee however you can."

"No," Plum said. "Not without you. And besides . . ."

"There is no besides. Just fly out of his reach."

"No," Plum said again.

The boy's voice rushed over them. "I'm gonna set you down on the ground, but please don't run away. I've got a bottle of water. I'll fill the lid for you and I won't touch you. Just let me look at you."

Crow's thoughts interrupted, though only Plum understood them. "She doesn't lap water like a cat!" He had struggled instinctively, and the boy's hand tightened. Crow stilled immediately.

"I'll keep my word," the boy said. They were lowered. Very, very slowly, the fingers relaxed and uncurled, withdrawn only slightly. "Don't run."

They didn't, though Crow's body trembled with the effort not to fight, not to grasp his dear friend by her garment and attempt escape.

"Be still, Crow," she said. "He'll not harm us."

The lid was placed inches away, and the sight of clear water flowing into it and over its rim was remarkably wondrous, because moonlight caught not only that liquid, but the almost invisible moisture rising from it into the night air, like the birth of millions of minute stars in a minuscule universe.

The boy's sigh was a warm sound to all of them.

Plum scooped water into her hand and sipped delicately, though she was thirsty enough to drop any pretensions to ladylike behavior, kneel and gulp. She wanted the boy to see her properly, as a refined, gracious creature, not at all meant for clutching and carrying off to dungeons.

Crow had edged sideways around the lid, keeping one eye always on the boy. Crow did look like a wild bird, feathers unkempt and dull, claws coated with soil. When he finished drinking, he backed up, keeping the position that allowed him to see both Plum and the boy. He spoke firmly, which the boy heard as "Caw! Caw!" and Plum heard as "We must leave. Now."

"I don't want to let you go," the boy said, "but I will. I gave my word." He sat up, a motion that caused brief turmoil in the wind, like a beginning storm. "But I hope you'll let me see you again. I wish you'd live here."

Plum and Crow looked at one another, sharing a moment of knowing: A wish had power.

Plum and Crow quickly assessed the house behind the boy. It was poorer even than the other family's, and with none of the little outer touches of a home. The porch roof sagged, which perhaps the family could not help, but a swing had broken slats and the chain hung unevenly—such small things could be repaired. A metal lawn chair lay on its side. No flowers or toys. And the windows—oh, there's darkness and there's darkness. Here no warmth seemed to wait within. Nothing radiated toward the glass. Nothing invited. No wonder the boy was out here in the midst of night, gazing at small wonders. He needed them.

"We can't live with you," Plum said gently, "but we will see you again. Keep your wits about you, and your eyes."

"Caw!"

"And," Plum translated, "never wish us harm."

Then Plum leapt onto Crow's good wing and scrambled

on his back as if the dear fellow would fly them both away. "Don't try to fly," she said. "Not yet." As his gait steadied, she sang a few lines of a song about willow trees and a young, sad boy. The moment she thought their captor could not see them well, she rose into the air and flew inches above Crow.

"I'll try now," Crow said, and managed a long half-flight leap, then another, and the last leap he flapped his wings, held straight ahead, and glided to their branch.

Plum sank beside him. "Crow is back," she said.

"Crow never left. Only one of his abilities weakened."

"True."

As Crow hunched down into a thick mass of tired ebony, Plum mused on their surroundings, which were no longer strange, but not familiar either.

"I have no idea what we're about," Plum said. "But I think we have no choice."

Shortly a tired voice said, "We have choice. That's what it's about."

"How do you know?"

"That I cannot answer. The moon is orange. You are beside me. I am tired. And we always have choice. I choose to sleep."

"Not I."

"Of course not."

She slept before he did, but she didn't know that. In her dreams she saw another creature much like herself, though plumper. The creature blew Plum a kiss and it tasted exactly like a berry! A blue, blue, ripe and wonderful berry. Berry? Sister? Friend? Plum made a sad sound, like a lonely sigh, and Crow moved his beak to brush her hair, attempting to leave the comfort of a human and loving touch.

· · ·

PLUM SAW her captor the next day—three times, actually— and once the day after, but, true to his word, he didn't pursue her.

"He may not have seen us," Crow said. "Or at least may not have seen *you*. It is difficult, you know, for humans to see anything out of the ordinary."

"Are you saying I do not compel attention?"

Crow recognized the teasing tone, but speaking of Plum so personally was a little emotional for him, especially being a crow with a crow's nature and highly fond of, deeply fond of, so very aware of this creature, the one now looking at him with her head back, throat velvet-white, lips parted. How could a human be beautiful to him?

He lowered the forepart of his body, as in a deep bow, and spoke from there. "You compel rapt attention." He raised up. "And the most exacting caretaking." He closed his eyes. "I must sleep."

Plum, too, slept, somewhat assured of safety not just because of Crow, but because the two humans who had seen her had not harmed her. In truth, they had shown no inclination to harm at all. Yet she had seen John harm creatures or almost harm them.

And had seen him become victim to the larger boy at the river. Oh! Humans were most complicated. She had much learning to do.

Since Crow had been insisting that he needed some brief times alone, Plum explored on her own. She learned the boundaries of the little town and the patterns of its citizens. The main street—and there was only one—was fairly deserted except for the lunch hour, when a few store or courthouse employees strolled to a place identified on a long, wooden sign above the entrance as "Bus Station." They ordered food that Plum envied, though she didn't know when, if ever, she had eaten it—chili, hotdogs, hamburgers.

The pungent smells, especially of onions, made her homesick for a home she didn't recall.

She found churches, a school—the latter empty now, but with wide windows through which she saw orderly books and desks, clean floors and blackboards, and recognized maps and globes. She was no stranger to any of this, and yet she was. When possible, unobserved, she entered stores and studied wares and customers. She scanned backyards, houses, became familiar with some pets, including the sturdy, sulky cat who had attacked a snake Plum's first day in this new world. She found and followed a meandering river that curled around the east and south sides of the town; found a factory with a shrieking whistle and with steam pumping out the chimney. From the factory's doors, a hundred or more women would pour at the end of the work-day, one of them John's mother. They were jolly women, though, laughing and hurrying as if home were a happy place in spite of hardship. John's mother was no exception. Just a few moments in the sun and she was smiling, striding up the hill toward the store, buying a few things for dinner, and then walking home. Sometimes John and Catherine would meet the mother and they would talk about various simple, but important things.

Plum discovered a fat woman who drove the town's one taxi. She was so huge, so obese, that the back seat of her car had been removed. With the exception of enough space for one slender passenger, she filled the car, but she was not ludicrous. She was popular, and her taxi—one side only inches from the pavement—was kept busy creeping from one place to another. Her cornsilk, short hair, which some people said was a wig, seemed too tiny a cap for such a woman, but suited the soft, unmarred white of her skin and the redness of her lips. Was she beautiful? people wondered. Why, yes. They supposed so. Just exceedingly heavy. But a nice woman. She and her work were respected.

Once Plum returned to Crow sooner than usual and found him swallowing something she didn't recognize. He became quite flustered and Plum, with a growing awareness of Crow's nature, said nothing, absolutely nothing, though so many remarks teased her lips that she turned pink with restraint. Now she realized why he might not have healed more rapidly. He needed enough of his own kind of nourishment.

She returned to contemplating her surroundings. The beauty of this little area of the country was astonishing. Was the whole world like this? Softened by light clouds, thick grass, morning dew, evening dew, mild night winds, sun-drenched breezes, rivers, birdsong. Could something be so wonderful it caused heartache?

"We'll have to leave someday, won't we?" Plum said to Crow.

"I don't know," he replied, adding in a sadder tone, "but I suspect so."

"Let's don't go," Plum asserted. "We'll just stay."

"We'll do what we must."

"Don't you ever weary of saying the proper thing? Your practical nature can be very burdensome, Crow. Did you ever think of that?"

"How could I not? After all, Miss Plum, it is I who most bears the burden of my nature."

Plum flitted away in indignation, admiration, and defeat.

WHEN PLUM WOKE, she lay in her bed listening, aware that some sound had disturbed her rest. She wasn't frightened since her tree-hollow home was secure. The tree had obviously sustained some injury long ago and grown past it, thriving despite this flaw—a flaw that was a blessing for Plum. She was particularly secure because Crow always kept post outside, somewhere near the entrance. A reliable friend, he would alert and defend her to the best of his ability. But whatever had awakened her wasn't Crow, and it wasn't a danger to herself or her friend. It was a stealthy sound, a movement not meant to attract any attention but attracting it for that very reason. What large creature crept at night but meant no harm?

Plum, having gone to bed in clean pantaloons and bodice, found her torn and soiled gown and stockings now intact and clean. She pulled the white silk stockings up to her knees, slipped the brocade gown over her head, lacing the front tightly, and finally slid her feet into new leather slippers resting beside her brocade boots. The attire was not that of a warrior, but unfortunately it was the only outfit she could dredge up, try as she would.

She stepped out her doorway slowly, on guard, her intelligent eyes assessing the surroundings. Crow was just stirring, perhaps aware of her. To the west of her tree the yard fanned out a gauzy silver, the effect of sharp moon on thick grass. And there, in the center of the yard, only a few feet from the woman's clothesline, was Catherine. Already pale-skinned, she seemed ghostly in the white nightgown and strange setting, and a chill ran through Plum. What, Plum wondered, was the child about? She was *so* thin. Plum thought this whole family should eat more, should indulge, should not hover so closely to need. The girl was rubbing liquid from the jar into her face, throat, and down her arms, and was speaking aloud, really chanting, almost a song. The words Plum couldn't distinguish, but she knew a ritual when she heard one. The girl was calling on a spirit or on magic or on something she *shouldn't* be contacting, as far as Plum was concerned.

"This can't be!" Plum shot forward, landing on the girl's outstretched hand and startling her so that she jerked away and ran to the house. Plum, herself shaken, turned to see someone fleeing across the neighboring yard while Crow landed beside her.

"What happened?" Plum asked, thinking it but also mouthing the words.

"We frightened more than the girl," came his response. "That fellow must have been watching the house and crept along the hedge to follow her."

"Did she see him? She'll be terrified."

Nearby was the jar, dropped in the girl's surprise. White liquid seeped into the soil. Plum came close, crinkled her nose. "Just milk?" she said, then crinkled her nose again. "Goat's milk. Now what was she trying to do?"

"Make her skin flawless?"

Plum remembered the girl in the kitchen, attempting to make her forearms smooth as a newborn's. "Of course!" she exclaimed. "Fancy you knowing that. She has freckles."

"Angel kisses."

"You're a treasure of surprises, Crow. Let's get you home."

"I can fare for myself." He lowered a wing to her, and Plum accepted, climbing gently to the back of his neck. He rose. His black feathers shone in the moonlight as if he glowed from within.

At their branch, Plum sat by Crow rather than enter her rooms. She did not want to find comfort yet, or sleep. Night sounds began again, the rustling of leaves, the whir of a small insect speeding by. It was lulling, since Plum was a being who slept nights. But she fought that sweet rest, letting her gaze return over and over to the house in which the girl and boy lived.

"I have to see if she is safe," she said.

"Of course, she's safe. She's inside for the night, as human children should be."

"But frightened, maybe, unable to sleep. No light has come on."

He didn't respond and she realized that her concern had awakened his. "You rest," she said.

"No. Where you go, I go. You'll get yourself killed."

"That's more likely to happen if you're stumbling around sick and wounded."

"I am no longer sick, my wound has healed, and I do not stumble. And who has saved whom?"

"Well said. But please?" She cocked her head much in his own fashion and he was so taken by the compliment and the grace that he acquiesced.

"I'll be listening. And you'll not have much time before I'm coming after you, walking if need be, though this has been a trial. I am meant, you know, to soar."

She bobbed her head solemnly. "As I know. Indeed. To soar."

And then Plum was off, on her own, though not far from Crow in any sense. By now, she knew the small house as if it belonged to her, and she wasted no time trying to find a chink to slip through. She sped to the front porch, hovered a tiny space from the doorbell, drew all her strength, and flew her tiny self into the button. She bounced some from the shock but heard the reward of the melody thus begun. So familiar. But she heard someone inside approaching the door and a muffled, "Who is it? Who's there? Argul?" Plum waited at the upper door-frame corner. At the precise moment the woman leaned forward to peer down the porch, Plum darted above the woman's head and into the house.

Plum experienced shame since the woman could then not go to bed and stayed in the living room, guarding her home against whatever. Plum maneuvered herself through the curtains into the bedroom. Ah! In the bed, the girl was curled on her side, eyes closed. The stiffness of her body and the absolute tightness of her lips gave her away—she was awake but hiding as children do when there's nowhere else to go, behind closed eyes. Plum stayed next to the meeting of wall and ceiling as she slowly and oh-so-silently flew toward the headboard, coming up on it from behind. She settled into a low, carved niche near the pillow and gave the child her whole attention.

The girl's breathing was audible and uneasy. She had not yet moved. In the close, warm bedroom, the smell of milk mixed heavily with a scent like flowers emanating from the girl's hair. She had, then, run straight to bed, without stopping to wash off the goat's milk. The thin points of her shoulders were slightly visible under the turn of sheet. Bits of moonlight briefly illuminated beads of moisture on the child's temple.

"Surranoo," Plum whispered, just a breath of sound, not at all like words. "Surranoo." Was it her imagination that the girl's tightness eased? "Yee're safe weeth me."

A second later, in one swift upheaval, the child sat up, grabbed something from the nightstand, turned over, clasped knees to chest, buried face against knees, and was totally still again. Except, of course, for a now troubled, quick breathing.

Plum wasn't leaving, let Crow worry what he would. Here she must stay, because whatever frightened the girl was not getting near her in fact or fancy. Plum sent thoughts to her friend, wondering, as she sat guard alone in this huge bedroom, dreary gray except for those minute pieces of moonlight that would always find their way inside, why children had to fear? Plum didn't know how such things came about, but she abhorred them. Yes. Hated them. And whoever caused or allowed them, too. "It is intolerable," she announced. "Unforgiveable."

The girl's eyelids fluttered, and Plum pressed her own willful lips together.

"Are you judging now?" she heard, most definitely from Crow. "And from what authority?"

"Me own!" she snapped, and Catherine's eyes opened completely. Words spilled from her mouth. "Now I lay me down to sleep, I . . ."

Oh! Plum herself had frightened the child! And now she saw what the girl clutched—a tiny Bible. Plum, remembering, glanced at the picture hung above the headboard—the angel guarding children.

She endured the completion of the prayer, and moments later, another recounting. Then another. How many times a night did the girl make her plea?

"Until she sleeps," Plum heard. This was, though, her own voice, her own words, her own thoughts.

So there they were, each of them feeling terribly alone, waiting for morning, or tomorrow, or something wonderful, like a pleasant hope or dream.

LESSONS BEGIN

"I calmed her, but then she suddenly feared again, perhaps me! I don't know how to help them," Plum said. "What am I supposed to do?" She had been agitated and pacing ever since arriving home a short time earlier. She would stride along the branch to her abode, then spin and stride toward Crow again. With each turn, her purple gown swirled and rustled, swirled and rustled. Nothing else in the world, Crow was certain, could make that exact, pleasing, feminine sound.

Though desperate to ease his friend's concern, Crow wasn't willing to give a quick answer. "First," he offered, "you might decide what they most *need*." Then, shifting his weight from one foot to the other, he ventured another suggestion. "Maybe *you* shouldn't make the decision. Maybe you should *ask*. No, no," he hastily corrected himself. "That won't do. Because they are proud, aren't they?"

"Of course."

"And proud people don't admit need."

Quick came her glance. "Are you talking about the family, Crow?"

"Who else?"

Plum let the small teasing go, turned again, paced, turned. The matter seemed urgent. "So what do I do?"

"You listen," Crow returned. "And you observe. And, when near enough, you whisper what they need to hear and ask what you need to know."

She had stopped walking. "I do talk to them. I soothe them. What more can I do?"

"You provide whatever they need that you have. Information. Experience."

"I have none."

"You chide me. Sometimes quietly and most forcefully."

"Not always appropriately."

"Yes. You must be more guarded with others. I know your ways."

Plum met his solemn black-eyed gaze. She felt more knowledge than she could express. "They weren't always kind."

"Thoughtless, not intentionally unkind."

Plum nodded. "Thank you."

"If you're hidden, you may even be able to speak aloud without alarming them. Your voice might not be a sound they can distinguish."

"But hear it?"

"Completely."

Plum pursed her lips, looked at the house, where the family most certainly would be stirring.

"I know the interior well now," she said. "I went through it very carefully this morning and found a way in and out. Well, actually, I *made* a way in and out."

"Big enough for me?"

"No. Not yet. But it could be. I'll show you later. I have, though, already learned something very important."

"What?"

"About our boy. Our little fisherman. His room is across from his mother's. It's very tiny, with no closet. He has many little things, not toys, but . . ."

"Collections?"

"Yes. Coins. Picture cards. Knives. And above his bed, the saddest thing."

"What? What?"

"A rifle, Crow. He has a rifle on a wooden rack above his head."

Crow, too, was dismayed. He lowered himself to the branch, sitting on his claws, as if he had gone weak. "A child? With a weapon?"

"I know," Plum said. She leaned into Crow's wing as she was wont to do when they were together like this. "So I have much talking to do, don't I?"

"Yes," he said. "And maybe I do."

"Maybe. After all, there's a sister, a brother, a mother."

"And," Crow added, "that Argul man."

"Yes."

"And," Crow also added, "that being who ran from the hedge last night."

"Oh! I had forgotten." She stepped back to look up toward his cocked head. "We can't do all this by ourselves," she cried. "We're not big enough."

"Speak for yourself," Crow said, but in a tone meant to jolly her, not to hurt her. "I am, for a Crow, quite huge."

"Well, you'll need to be," Plum said. "Because I'm not large. Not at all. I've never, ever, felt so small."

"Rhyme intended?"

"Why not? If I can't order the world, then I'll order my speech."

"Caw!" came his laughter and delight. "Caw! Click. Click. Rattle."

· · ·

NOW PLUM'S days were organized around the life of the human family. School had begun, and each morning the children rose very early, ate breakfast in the warm, bright kitchen, then accompanied their mother to the factory where she began work at exactly 7:15 by the factory whistle time. The children stayed in the anteroom of the factory, where sometimes other children also waited. Shortly before 8:00, the little troop would leave, walking quite orderly to the school grounds not far beyond. Plum never returned to the tree and yard until her humans were well occupied, safely inside a building, at studies. Then she set about her own duties: polish her skills, acquire more abilities, particularly making things appear when needed. What was the good of being a witch if the only power one had was flight? Of course, her gown had a bit of its own magic, she supposed. How else did it restore missing sections, faded color, rips, and even bodice lace? The sleeves, which would become slack and droopy, would overnight be puffed again, as if newly made. Shoes, of course, the slippers and boots, simply provided.

One afternoon Plum removed her gown, put it on a hanger fashioned from willow twigs, hung it on a wall hook of rose-briar thorn and then, dressed in pantaloons and camisole, sat on the bed and tried to make the gown renew itself before her very eyes. Nothing changed, though by sheer concentration alone her weary eyes had made the room seem aglow, wavery, as if she saw it through a veil. But blinking a few times dispelled the illusion and there hung the stubborn gown, a bit limp, the luster gone.

"Then fall!" Plum demanded, impatient as always. "If you won't mend yourself before me, then fall! Fly! Disappear!" She waved her arm as if she were royalty dismissing an underling. A voice caught her attention. She hurried to her arched doorway, hearing Crow's thought as she saw him. "Look what I brought you."

"Bread? White bread!"

"I thought this would please you." Crow carefully maneuvered the slice of bread onto the branch.

Even lying flat, the bread was waist-high to Plum. To her, this was no morsel.

"It tears easily," Crow said.

"You needn't worry about me. I've just never seen it this way." Plum placed her hands on the crust, her expression one of surprise and pleasure, perhaps even awe. "Up close," she whispered, "it's almost like crystal." She placed her hand into the hollow of an air bubble. "It's not solid at all, Crow, nor flat, nor plain. To be so soft, it captures the air itself. I couldn't do that."

"No," Crow thought, "nor I. But neither do I want to."

Plum laughed and so did Crow. Their blended voices were like the rich warble of a beautiful creature, perhaps a waterwing. They ate together slowly, appreciating the bread as food and as more than food.

"We will need to store up for winter," Crow said. "If you would tell me what you need, or," he nodded toward the house across the span of yard, "they need, I'll see what I can do. Of course, I, too, am limited. He shuffled a step away. "Though I can steal. Obviously."

"It's in your nature, right?"

"Truly. Not a choice. As a crow, no choice."

They looked at one another. His last statement implied he had once been other than a crow. But nothing else came to them.

"You don't have to steal," Plum said. "I'll think on this. There must be a way. I am, after all, a witch."

Crow moved even farther away.

"Where are you going?"

"Where I can think more deeply and clearly."

"Must it be away from me?"

There was a moment before he said, "Yes, my dear. It must. Your thoughts too often overpower my own."

What could Plum make of that? When had she overpowered him? Had she once dismissed him? A sadness swept through her, a knowledge almost remembered. "Leave me," she had said, in different ways. And so he had.

Plum tried to stay with the children most of the time. Certain hours inside the home were lovely, like picture book stories, fairy-tale families. While the mother prepared dinner, the daughter helped or sat at the table, listening. The mother talked about her workday, how fast the women could sew, but never fast enough to please the St. Louis boss. The manager was nice enough, but he had to raise the quota and it made money so hard to earn.

Often the mother expressed her hope that Catherine would have a good life, and warned her never to work in a factory, and never to live in misery. "You can always leave, she said, "even if you have to walk."

Catherine's eyes revealed the pain such talks caused her. Children who have unhappy parents don't want the parents to leave and don't want to leave themselves. Oh no! "They want to fix things," Plum fumed aloud. "And they can't! Because they're so little!" Oh, oh, what could she do?

The mother didn't always talk about the factory, but most of her stories were of troubles too sad for young ears. She talked of her own mother's death, of the stepmother—a truly mean woman, but one who had also had an unhappy life.

Plum liked best when the mother sang. Those song-stories were sad, too, but the voice was itself a pleasure. Plum understood why Catherine would say, "Sing, Momma. Sing 'Redwing'" or "Sing 'The Butcher's Daughter.'" When the kitchen filled with that pure, sweet, plaintive voice, the door of John's room would open and he would join them. The kitchen table was small, metal, with a top that mimicked a red-checkered cloth. But when the three were in the room, it truly looked like a red-checkered cloth. Though Plum knew that music had no color, still she felt the mother's singing was like sunshine in the small room, made it glow almost golden from warmth, made it an old-fashioned memory just being fashioned.

At bedtime, each family member retired to a separate room for sleep and dreams. Plum waited while the girl performed all the little acts that were somehow important to her: folding her clothing just so, placing her barrettes in the exact spot on the dresser, so they pointed toward the opposite corner, putting her shoes side by side halfway under the bed, clean socks lying across the arch. These were rituals, maybe for safety. Last came her prayers, always repeated at least three times, then a long, miserable time when her small body was rigid, her breathing irregular. Sometimes sweat beaded her young brow.

This night, Plum, huddled at first in the headboard carving, directed all her thoughts and caring toward the child. "You are safe," Plum thought, "safe for the night, safe always with me. Safe, sweet Catherine, safe. No one will harm you. No one." Plum moved down to the pillow, wishing she were as big as the mother now, and able to stroke the child's red curls. She recalled Crow's admonishments, to offer more than comfort. She rethought the mother's remarks, which Plum had considered too harsh, and tried to understand what the mother meant and what Catherine heard. Then she turned her mind to the troubled girl beside her: "Your mother will not leave you. She doesn't want to leave here and she doesn't want you to leave. She's giving you freedom to flee unhappiness if you wish to or need to. But you may choose to stay. Always.

You have your own heart, Catherine, and will make your own choices. Now, because you are young, you should remain where you are, loved and safe. Life is good! You are good! You may trust yourself."

In John's room, Plum sat on a bedpost knob at the head of the bed and thought toward the sleeping John: "You are precious. Dear and precious to your sister, to your mother, to me, to the world." She glided down and sat on the edge of his pillow. "Be kind, John, be kind to all creatures. Hurt nothing unless you must in order to save yourself or to save someone else. Forgive those who injure you but don't tolerate injury. Be kind to others and kind to yourself. Don't become like those you dislike." Plum had almost said "hate" but she didn't want to allow the word to exist between them.

She was pleased that John slept easily, rarely moving. Nighttime for him was a time of rest, which puzzled Plum. Then she thought of the answer: The boy's terrors came only when *others* were in this home, and the boy felt different from them all. Especially The Argul.

Plum wanted to understand John and Catherine. She listened to their conversations—really just short exchanges—with other children who waited at the factory, or with fellow classmates at school. John was so sweet, shy. Other children liked him, for which Plum was grateful. He seemed happy in school—and he was quite a good student. His printing was straight and even, though small, and he would erase and rewrite any wayward letter. His penmanship book was the best in the class, if Plum did say so herself. Perhaps, she told Crow, the letters were a little too perfect. "Like small soldiers," she said. "He controls them deftly." She made a quick erasing moment.

"He is a small destroyer."

"That is a harsh word for a child's action."

"I stand corrected."

Plum was so taken aback by her easy victory, she could say nothing but "Yes."

Later, she realized Crow had won. He had been sincere, not witty.

JOHN PLAYED MOSTLY with one particular boy. They would talk about fishing or hunting, as though they were grown men and very experienced. They talked about skinning a squirrel, which alarmed Plum so much she became nauseated, though it was evident neither boy had ever done such a thing. She stayed out of sight but made such an angry "bizzzzzzzzzzIT, bizzzzzzzzzzIT" sound that John, with a careful look around, said gently, as if for overhearing ears as well as for his playmates, "Let's go inside. The bell's about to ring." He had recognized her distress.

The other boy was looking around, too, and stopped to glance behind them. John, as if he might have been the source of the sound, said "bizzzt." He then hid a very charming smile which Plum, now perched on the cutout of an owl above the blackboard, didn't miss. The little scoundrel. The darling dear. Another day when his playmate sighted his slingshot at a wren, a homely, tiny bird, John said, "Don't," in his husky little voice, and Plum took a deep breath, feeling an oddly maternal pride.

Below, the playmate defended his desire. "Why not? It's just a wren."

"It's not hurting you."

The boy pulled the sling taut, as if to shoot anyhow, and John spun on his heel and walked away. His friend, with one puzzled glance at John's back, let the pellet loose toward a low spot on the trunk, far from the unsuspecting wren.

"Hey!" the boy called, running after John. "Want to go over to the high school later?"

Plum learned that, at the school for the bigger children, John and his friend only observed. If a baseball game or track meet were underway, they'd sit not in the bleachers, but along the sidelines, where sometimes a coach or kid would say, "Get out of the way."

John studied most closely the boys who had taunted him at the river that summer day, particularly the tall one who had broken his rod. John's expression wasn't one of anger or fear; perhaps curiosity. And something else.

"Loneliness," Plum reported to Crow. "Maybe even respect. Though why would anyone respect a bully?"

"Fear of strength is a kind of respect, whether of friend or foe."

"Oh! I have me a philosopher Crow!"

"Well done, to match with rhyme."

"I know."

Studying Catherine was an entirely different matter, because in the area of girlhood, Plum was much more experienced, or at least believed she probably was. She saw how Catherine tried to shorten herself by not standing erect; how she tried to disguise the thinness of her straight, healthy legs by always crossing them when sitting, or, when standing, by wrapping one foot around the other ankle to keep one leg indistinguishable—or so she thought—from the other. Even her long, slender, competent fingers were unpleasing to her, and she shaped her hands into fists, hiding the thumbs by slipping them beneath the curled fingers.

"This child is going to disguise herself into absolute nonexistence," Plum spouted to Crow. "I don't think she likes one detail of her fine little person. Not her hair, her skin, her nails, her brow, her eyes. You know what she did, Crow? You know what she did?"

"I most certainly will know momentarily, will I not?"

"She burned matches in the restroom, then rubbed the blacking against her lashes."

"How novel."

"It is not novel, but old art, and not for such a young girl. She went home with such streaks under her eyes that she looked like a chimney sprite."

"A what?"

Plum had fallen silent, amazed at her own words.

"A what?" Crow repeated.

"A chimney sprite," Plum whispered. "Whatever that is."

"I think you know."

"I think I do, too, but it's hiding somewhere in here." She placed her fingertips to her temple.

"A most wonderful place to hide."

But Plum was lost in thought, trying to capture a memory that had faster flight than she.

While Plum learned her family's woes and answered them as best she could, Crow guarded the night yard. He did not sleep. His sharp eyes caught every slight movement, even the variation of shadow. He heard nightbirds crying, frogs croaking, crickets singing, heard cats and raccoons prowling, dogs roaming. But the natural movements of night didn't concern him. Crow was listening and looking for something else, for the hulking human who had been behind the hedge, who had run into the shadows. Crow was going to thwart that creature's plan, if the creature were up to no good. And who could be planning something pleasant while hiding in the murky midnight? Caw! Caw! Come on, fellow. Crow awaits.

One night later, when thunderclouds veiled the moon and wind whisked leaves away in thick waves, Crow heard a loud motor, a car obviously speeding through the small town. It neared and Crow attended closely, prepared for flight or fight. As he feared, the car slid to a stop in front of this house, his and Plum's house, their family's house, and Crow shot like a winged arrow toward the vehicle. There, a tall, lean man was already out.

"I'm not afraid to knock. I don't care what time it is." He turned toward the porch, striding a little unsteadily toward it. "Hey, Argul! Hey buddy! Let's party. Get yourself out here! The night is young!"

From behind him came men's laughter, and a hooting sound, though none of this was funny at all, certainly neither to Crow nor Plum, who was already in the curtain fold, waiting for the mistress of the house to open the door, which she did, but stayed behind the screen door to speak.

"I know you, Walter Conrad." She hadn't turned on any lights but had donned a soft robe of pink chenille. She herself looked so young, her fair skin smooth in the shadows. "You go on home to your family."

"Want to talk to Argul. He's my buddy."

"Argul's not here. And even if he were, this is no time to get a husband and father out of bed."

"We all want to see Argul."

She didn't answer.

"He said he'd be here."

"Yeah!" came from someone in the car, and a paunchy man emerged. This form was one Crow recognized. He shot down toward the car in a tight swoop, and up against the man's face, not pecking or scratching, just swooping, like a firm shadow. Again. And again.

"Damn. You see that? Damn! Again! That's a crazy bird. Maybe it's rabid!"

The woman stepped onto the porch, and a second later the tall fellow close to her ducked and swatted the air. "Dang! What is that?"

The woman, too, was amazed. She herself had done nothing.

The man who had squealed yanked the car door open. "Let me in. Scoot over! Scoot, I tell you!"

"Something's after Walt, too!"

Walt was now climbing into the passenger seat of the front, and the back door was being slammed by the big man, who then began slapping at the glass where the bird appeared again, while the driver put the car in gear and took off.

"Something bit me," Walt said, "or stung me." He rubbed his cheek.

"Tell me about it. Did you see that damned bird?"

"Wasn't a bird that got me. Maybe a spider. Something sharp. They're poisonous. Birds aren't."

The car careened down the road, fleeing what, the men didn't know.

Inside the house, Plum balanced on the curtain rod spanning the double door of Catherine's bedroom. From there, Plum could see both woman and daughter, in separate rooms, both in anguish. The woman was seated on her sofa, face buried in her palms. Catherine stood silently behind the heavy, green curtain, obviously concerned about her mother, but uncertain what to do, how to comfort. She was so slender, and against the draped fabric, seemed even slighter, like the folds might wrap around her and she'd disappear forever, pale, sweet thing. John, on whom Plum had also checked, had been up since the first voice called, and was seated on his bed, rifle across his lap.

Feeling overwhelmed, Plum knew she could be of no help this evening. They would all be uneasy. Still, she wouldn't leave until in the smallest, low-set bedroom, John had stood unsteadily on the bed and placed the rifle across the hooks. Such a monstrous thing to mark a wall above a child's sleep.

But. If it made a child feel safe? Oh, who could make careful, right decisions when more than one could bear the cost?

Plum needed rest. In the kitchen, alone, she slid between the loose door of the old flue, now turned into a narrow wall cupboard from ceiling to floor, but still called the flue. On the very bottom, she ran to the right back corner and lifted the curling wallpaper, scooting into the hole behind it. The creature who had gnawed it was long gone, or at least Plum had not yet seen it. In the narrow between-walls, she dropped down to the underhouse and flew slowly, just a few inches above the untrodden soil, to the latched door of the crawlspace. There, at the very bottom, a broken corner of wood allowed her to squeeze out. She was at the back of the house, but flew quickly up, up, over the roof, her thought calling Crow. In seconds, he was beside her, alighting on the highest pitch of the roof.

Crow's mind was roiling, angry, frightened, concerned. That was the man! That one! He who had been peeking at the girl! How many times had he lurked to spy on her? Monster! Oh, Crow was ready. Anytime.

"Don't!" Plum said, responding to Crow's thoughts. "You may frighten him, or anyone when necessary. But no real harm."

"Are you all right?"

"Did you hear my remark? No harm to anyone."

"I heard it."

"You are the most exasperating crow."

"How many of us do you know?"

She turned away briefly, because even in the aftermath of a terrible misery, she was almost won to smiling. And she didn't believe that to be appropriate. "You were very brave, Crow. Very."

He peered off into the blackness where the men had sped. "I had some harm planned." He shifted his weight to one claw, stretching the other.

"Stop that! You may not hurt anyone seriously. I forbid it."

"Do you now?"

"I said *seriously*. Don't harm him seriously. Not his eyes."

"You heard that? Are no thoughts my own?" He stepped inches away, stretching low and forward so he might be on her level. With his head right before her, both eyes trained on her, he vowed, "I won't cause *you* pain and thus will not do to others more than what I must."

She placed her hand on his beak, on the pure ebony of it.

He waited.

"Well said."

He dipped his head a fraction more, and reared back to his normal, grand posture. After a moment or so of lovely silence together, he thought, "And you, Plum? I heard one of those men squeal. The one nearest the house. The sound was most pleasing."

"I didn't hurt him, not really. Just small. A small hurt. A wee, wee wound."

"How wee? What kind of wound? Plum?"

"Let's go home. I'm weary."

"Plum. We are establishing rules here."

"Very well. I have to wash out my mouth."

"Your mouth? You bit him!"

"I did." Her slender hand now cupped her mouth, as if to keep the confession still secret. "Oh, Crow, I did. Twice!"

"Mercy," Crow said, though his pleased tone did not match the word. He lifted, turned in a graceful circle above his friend. "How nice." He rose higher, circled again, a lovely arc that was momentarily outlined against the moon before he disappeared in the blacker sky.

"How nice, how nice, how nice," Plum thought she heard, like a soft melody.

It did not, however, remove the distaste of her action nor the ugly taste in her mouth. She needed a saltberry paste. A strong one. Ohhh. She shuddered.

Plum, weary to her depths, flew home, and noticed only vaguely that Crow had not yet arrived. She retired to her rooms. She removed her gown and shoes, and in the light of moonstones studied herself in the small mirror.

"Flimsy creature," she whispered. "A strong breath could undo you, yet you think to help others?" Her voice lapsed into the internal dialect she shared with Crow. "Summa mad yeee taeny, e eef yeee cud nae ficht tha, wha hooop tae ficht fae oothurs?" In the wavery light her mirror self seemed equally ashamed of its size and nature. Plum closed her eyes. She sank into sleep.

And dreamed—about a young lady much like her but with auburn hair, no freckles, and with a sweet-sounding name, one that rolled pleasantly from the lips, that made one happy to say or recall or dream of. A good name, delicate. A friend's name. What? What was it? In her sleep, Plum turned over, her lips forming a letter, a letter—B. She smiled, still in dream. Berry. Berry. Sweet Berry. Tart Plum. Do you know where you come from?

Her eyes fluttered open. What had she remembered? She sat up. Berry! Who was Berry! This was no dream. This was a memory!

In her joy and excitement Plum ran out into the night, calling for Crow. She almost glimmered on the branch, so dark was the evening and so white her undergarments. She wanted to wing herself somewhere immediately—into the past, the future, wherever she had to be to know everything! Everything! "Crow! I have a past!" She continued calling till the cooler night air made her shiver and, with a fond but worried glance toward the little house and wherever Crow must be, she returned to her own abode. There she prepared to bathe in the natural alcove that now held a clamshell braced by the two clear stones Crow had given her. They emitted heat if she put her hand near them and ceased if she repeated the gesture. She filled the clamshell with stored rainwater and dew, and while it warmed, she tied her wild curls up and disrobed. She trembled from the hope of memories returning and foretelling the future.

Crow, leaving Plum to rest, had immediately gone in search of the car full of villains. He was soon successful, for crows are swift and fierce, and he recognized the hunched metal lurching down the highway like a dying beetle, though without, of course, that creature's dignity. The men in this car were drunk, and belonged at home, if not in a dismal cave somewhere, shut away where they could not cause others pain or unhappiness.

Though Crow could not pull down his brows, still he frowned as he trailed the miserable men. How to get them off the road? What skill did Crow have? Rocks! Glass! Shards! He would give them stony rain. Let them fear even the sky when Crow was aloft. Ha! Off he went—actually, down he dropped—to gather in beak and claws pebbles of various small sizes. Then, struggling under this self-imposed heavy load, he rose again. He wanted, of course, to drop all his ammunition at once, for the effect—and the pleasure— but he didn't want to direly harm anyone by causing a wreck, and, to boot, have to face an indignant, righteous two-inch wrath. He had to be quite careful. So Crow continued holding the pebbles in beak and claws, a very awkward state, until the car slowed down, apparently prepared to drive into Buxton proper. Then, more than relieved at the opportunity, Crow let the beakful loose and followed that with a stone stream first from one claw and then the other. If crows could smile, he did so. The moonlight glinted off his beak and at the very least made a shadow mimic a smile. He curved down, low, made a quick landing to gather more pebbles and returned to his higher vantage. The car had stopped! The driver was half-in, half-out, peering up and around.

Crow flapped madly above the man, deliberately drawing his attention, then dropping all the pebbles at once. He wished he had more! More! They clattered sweetly on the hood and top of the car.

"It's that crazy bird again!" The man disappeared inside the vehicle, the door slamming behind him. The car chugged into motion, then careened onto the gravel.

Oh no! Crow had erred! He was furious with himself. Now the men would speed into town.

But Crow also had succeeded. The driver let out first one man, then another, pausing in front of houses only long enough to allow each to clear his body from the car. Crow followed along, noting where each man lived, especially the big man, the hulk, the lurker.

That man, on emerging from the vehicle, leaned down to the driver's window. "Argul's boat must've gotten off schedule."

"Or he changed his mind. He had thought about going to Canada between shifts this time."

"He owes me money."

"Who doesn't he owe? He's a good sort, though."

Grunt.

Crow watched the heavy monster go into its own house, and for a moment Crow considered staying on his perch, keeping this creature in his field of vision. But instead, feeling duty-bound to mark the origin of each man, he followed the car and its driver to the final stop.

And Crow was glad he had done so. Instinct had served him well. Because this house he knew. The boy who had been his and Plum's captor lived within. The final drunk man, who now meandered toward the porch, was the boy's father.

No wonder that child, too, needed a witch and crow in his life. No wonder that child, too, longed for magic and beauty.

Crow alighted, landing atop the now empty car. When the front door opened and the man emerged, Crow spread his wings and the man hied himself back into the house. Moments later, the door opened and a barefoot young man in pajama bottoms hurried toward the car.

"Caw!" Crow announced.

"You're here!" He glanced over his shoulder. "You'd better take off."

"CAW!" Not on your life.

"My dad's getting my BB gun."

"CAW!" Send him out.

But the boy had opened the car door, grabbed something, and was running to the house. "Pa! Got 'em." He disappeared inside.

Crow waited, gaze fixed on the door. Let the man come! Coward! Sending a child.

He waited a long time. In fact, his head was drooping and his bottom feathers were near the cold metal. He was about to sit and sleep. The door opened again, very quietly, and the boy emerged.

"You there?" the child's voice whispered.

"Caw!" Yes.

The boy had taken one cigarette from his father's pack for himself. When, on the street side of the car, he struck the match to light the cigarette, Crow clutched it in one claw, dropped it to the gravel, and squelched the flame with one firm claw blow. Then he went after the cigarette, but the boy, amused and not at all afraid, had put it in his pocket.

"Worse than my mother," he said.

Crow landed next to him, in the dusty gravel. "CAW!" He was no woman.

The boy understood the attitude, though he heard

nothing but "Caw!" He would have put his arms around his buddy, but how does a boy hug a Crow?

"I wonder what you think about," the boy said. "I wonder if you know you're a crow, if you know you're a bird at all."

Crow stretched his neck upward, spread his wings elegantly.

"I see. You *do* know." The boy looked up, squinting as if to focus on something not too visible. "Where's the little fairy woman?"

Crow stayed perfectly still, as though he did not understand.

"I wouldn't hurt her. It's just . . . It's the kind of thing I'd like to know was real. It's a sort of . . . present. Like a birthday or something. Only you find it or it finds you."

Crow had to remain quiet. He had to. Though he was very touched by the boy's need, and understood it well, Plum's presence was not his to reveal or to assure and certainly not to give. He must be a stoic Crow. All he could give was himself.

In a moment, after closely watching Crow, the boy said, "Okay." He nodded, reached for the cigarette. Crow hopped to his shoulder. It was a precarious perch, but a necessary one. He bent down, thrusting his beak into the shirt pocket just ahead of the boy's hand.

"All right. You win." The boy laughed, and Crow, cigarette in beak, flew off. "Tomorrow night," he heard following him. "Please? Tomorrow night?"

Then, faintly, a woman's voice, also from that spot below. "Paul? Honey, get in this house. What are you doing?"

Crow was uncertain what to do with the burden he now carried. He couldn't drop it somewhere unplanned, because it might poison water, or ground, or some other creature. He'd think on it tomorrow. He flew home, pinioning the cigarette on a broken twig on the other side of their tree.

Outside Plum's door, he stood listening for a few moments. She was there, because his sensitive ears caught the sound of her soft breathing. And from that rounded room came such a rich blend of scents, strawberries and melon and warm honey, that he felt almost intoxicated, from pleasure in life if not from aromas alone. He moved inches away, studying the high moon, the humble house, the expanse of yard. The cool night breeze ruffled his chest feathers. He felt strong. Responsible. Manly. Crowly? His lot in life was so peculiar. He could not place himself. But he loved Plum. He remembered loving her.

In the morning, Plum and Crow had much to share, but little time. They took a brief flight together, zooming between the light blue heaven and the gold and russet earth, their senses filled with the change of seasons, and with their own experiences. Crow brimmed with words about Paul; Plum about Berry.

"My clan cared for trees and plants," Plum said. "I know that."

"And mine cared for animals," Crow replied. "We were ill-matched."

"Who dared say that?" from Plum.

"I believe the word was never spoken aloud," replied Crow.

"I believe we were fay folk," Plum said, stepping back to better see his reaction.

He bent toward her, his head turning, so he somewhat curled around her. She felt embraced. As he rose seconds later, she heard, "I believe we are."

How much they wanted to know. How little they knew, and how slowly it came. Is home near here? Across the ocean? Where in time? How to go back?

"Maybe we will find ourselves there if we do the right thing."

"Such as?"

"We'll know when it happens."

"If!" Plum cried, and quickly regretted the harshness. They were together. If they had been parted once, they could be again.

As they circled the outskirts of the small town, Crow veered briefly north. "I've been there," he said turning back. To the north a ridge of higher land crossed toward the southwest. "It seemed familiar. Not home, but similar."

Plum hovered, scanning the distant hills. "Should we go?"

"No. As I said, it's not home. Besides, we have a task."

Something else was in the air. It had to do with pumpkins, carved to resemble grinning monsters, with replicas of ghosts hanging from trees and bushes, with false gauzy spider webs appearing on porches, hedges, in windows. Even along the short main street of town decorations hung like banners proclaiming a world of witchery and wonder.

They arrived at the plum tree. What was about? Each knew but was unable to grasp the exact memory. Then Plum, standing on their favorite peering branch and smelling, quite oddly, a rich tobacco scent, suddenly recaptured the word.

"Halloween!!" she proclaimed.

"All Saint's Eve!" Crow responded.

"Not today?"

"No. But soon."

"Yes," Plum said. "Soon. Perhaps tomorrow."

"Or the next day."

"Or the next."

They were breathless, and why not? A battle had been fought and won and more were to come. They had each other and they had three charges—responsibilities accepted wholeheartedly. Plum slipped her right hand between the dense black feathers of Crow's left wing. It was much like the intermingling of fingers. Both felt warm and comforted.

Their world was becoming immense.

"Well," Plum said. "My family waits."

Crow prepared to fly. "And so does mine."

Plum hesitated. "What is that smell? It's pungent."

"Tobacco. Most horrible. I'll dispose of it when I can think how."

"No. Don't. I find it very pleasant."

"What?" Crow stayed on the branch, perplexed at this unseemly pleasure from such an otherwise almost perfect creature. He watched Plum descend near the rickety gate-door to the crawlspace beneath the house and disappear. She was about her work and he must be about his. He took flight.

THE WONDER OF BOYS AND GIRLS

*P*lum made her way into the house and into the mother's bedroom. There, Plum walked slowly across a glass-topped box. Hand-painted on the glass was a dense bouquet of blossoms, all various shades of purple and blue. Since the box's wooden sides rose an inch above the glass, and were intricately curved, Plum could be almost invisible if she were cautious in her movements and if no one looked directly at her. The woman wasn't in the room; her daughter was. Catherine sat before a low vanity dresser and fashioned her unruly hair in different upsweeps. None apparently pleased her and she shook her head vigorously. "Ragmop," she muttered. "Ragmop! Ragmop!" She opened a small drawer to her right and, after a quick glance toward the curtained doorway, examined the drawer's contents—her mother's meagre collection of makeup over the years. She took out a small bottle, uncapped it, and by repeatedly applying fingertip first to upended bottle, then to face, placed rows of dots across cheekbones, brow, down nose, cheek, and neck. She rubbed the dots together, creaming the liquid into her pale skin, then leaned to the mirror, so close her breath glazed the glass. She retrieved the bottle once more and repeated the process. Now she was certainly a darker-skinned child. Then came a lip balm, which was too pale to please her. She found, far in the back of the drawer, a very small tin, removed the top and was obviously pleased. Here was a worthy color. Carmine. She applied it to her lips which thus became quite hideous—too red, too shapeless. When she tried to wipe off the red, it instead spread across her upper lip and onto her cheek. She had to wet her fingertips and still it would not fade away.

Rouge, Plum decided. The child had found not lip balm but rouge pot. Unused and dried. So now more dots of the cream liquid were applied, wiped, applied again, and the mouth and cheek were more in keeping with the rest of her features, though a faint flush underlay the skin.

Next came penciled dark eyebrows, far too straight, too long. Plum knew this was no costume the child was crafting. It was herself.

Shortly, after fluffing her red curls up and out and stretching them in an unruly tumble, Catherine stood, replaced the vanity stool, and with one final glance at herself, left the room. Plum, so concerned with the child's growing dissatisfaction, followed rapidly, almost colliding with the hair halo when the girl stopped short. The back door was opening, someone was humming—the mother was inside the house again. The girl ran lightly, but not soundlessly, to her own room, leaving the curtains swaying heavily and Plum thus shut out. Even the breeze from the curtains' movement was rather powerful to Plum's tiny form. She was not, after all, a bee.

Here came the mother. Up shot Plum. And apparently a light shaft had revealed her, for the woman, now inside the living room, holding an empty clothes basket in her hand, was peering right at Plum! Directly. There on the wood frame of the curtained entrance into the child's room.

"My Lord!" the woman said. "What is that thing? Get the flyswatter."

Plum dropped onto her belly and felt her dress skirt billow up.

"It's a bumblebee," came John's voice. "I'll get it."

"You'll do no such thing. You stay away from that thing. Get me the swatter."

Plum had squinched shut her eyes and thought "Crow!" as loudly inside as she was capable of doing, but she knew that was foolish. He could not possibly arrive soon enough or enter the home or— What happened?

She opened her eyes only a bit, not yet moving. Though still lying face down, and still on a high perch, she was no longer in the living room. She was in the boy's room! Atop the gun! On the barrel!

Up she sat, and John saw her. He had taken an empty jar from his closet instead of going for the flyswatter his mother wanted, and now stood with the jar in one hand, its lid in the other.

"I thought it was you," he whispered. His lips had that sweet curl on one side. "Get in." He held the jar out and she flew right to it, lighting on the back of his hand first and letting him observe her closely.

"John Ivan!" came from the living room. "It's loose somewhere. Get the swatter."

He smiled again and Plum slid down his bent fingers into the glass. He lifted the top of the hollow step by his door and placed the jar inside. "You'll be safe here," he said. Then he went into the hall. Sound and light came through gaps in the crudely constructed step. Plum listened.

"If you'll open the doors," John said, "it'll probably fly out."

"I don't want it to fly out," the mother said. "I've never

seen a bee like that. Besides, if it flies out, it can fly back in again. I think I'd rather have it dead."

"You think fishing is cruel. Killing is worse."

The mother didn't answer.

Plum stayed in the jar, waiting for John, because no telling what else he had locked away in here. It might be something that liked bees or two-inch witches. While she waited, she pondered her shift from the living room into this room. How had she done that? Just how? First, she was on her stomach. Yes. And then she closed her eyes. Yes. She had transported herself.

Maybe she could transport herself again. She stretched out on the jar bottom. She closed her eyes. She squinched them. But when she peeked, the curve of the glass and the wood beyond were still there. She sat up. What else had she done on that ledge? Ummmm. Been afraid? Perhaps. But could one will fear? Simply bring it up when needed? Perhaps need was the clue. True need.

When the boy came after her later, creaking the step's top upward, Plum was amazed that from her lower vantage point he could appear so huge. Of course, he was many, many times her size, but usually she viewed him from a higher vantage, or at least an equal horizontal one. But from the ground? Looking up as he bent toward her? Gigantic. The curve of the glass jar contorted his features and he became a hideous sky, one with eyes and nose and mouth, flesh colored and lowering, lowering. As she took a gasping breath, the thought flashed that now she would disappear again.

But she didn't.

John's words were like a fresh, slow, nicely scented breeze. "I'll take you outside now. Don't let her see you again." He carried her through the dim kitchen, where a clock light was like a planet of time, into the laundry room, and out the back door. He carried her all the way down the yard, right to her tree. He almost tipped her out but stopped himself just as the jar tilted. Instead, he dropped to his knees and laid the jar on its side.

Plum walked out.

He sat back on his heels.

She nodded as though descending velvet-covered stairs. "Thank you."

He nodded.

She pursed her lips, though that did not make her one whit taller. "What is your full name?" she asked, straining to speak loudly and still melodiously, as a young woman witch should.

"John Ivan Hobbson."

She accepted the name with a regal half-nod and fulfilled her part of the exchange with "Plum."

She flew straight up. She assumed he smiled. Young males had an odd proprietorial and amused air about women who were their elders if not their betters.

On her tree branch again, she breathed deeply of night air, cool, and wanted to race high, higher, in search of adventure and beauty. Where was that Crow? Then a mild acrid scent caught her attention. Tobacco. She neared the pinioned cigarette. This, too, was memory. Nice. Rich.

Off to find Crow—at the captor Paul's, she was sure.

Crow was atop the corrugated roof of a small shed. The metal ripples were like chutes, each filled with decaying leaves and moisture. Rusty and muddy water—or a similar liquid—oozed down the ripples and dripped erratically along the sides of the shed. From inside the crude construction came a familiar voice, Paul's, and occasional responding voices. His cronies? His gang? The tormenting horde?

"What are they planning now," Plum asked. "More meanness to our John?"

"No. They are planning costumes for the coming witches' night."

"I see." But she laughed. She wasn't opposed to pretense and posing by young men, just to unkindness.

"Is anyone going as a Crow?"

"Why, yes. How astute."

"They are not. You're teasing."

He huffed, but he also relented and there came that odd quirk of expression that seemed almost a smile, though crows absolutely cannot smile. Their anatomical structure will not allow it.

"Actually," Crow said, "no one is going as a crow. But no one is going as a witch either."

"They are then?"

"One ghost, two pirates, two hobos, and a gambler."

"A gambler?"

"Paul found a black armband and is determined to use it."

"That's a *grieving* band."

"Not if one is gambling."

"How would you know?"

Crow tilted his head, and Plum prepared herself. "Well?" she said.

"In my own way, my dear Plum, I am a game bird."

She laughed sharply, fully, happily. She plopped down, and her skirt swooshed out over the edge of a ripple, where it soaked up a brown stain, and even that sight couldn't lessen her fine humor.

Both she and Crow realized that the group inside the shed had fallen silent. Crow assumed the boys were utterly captivated by the sound of humor shared, though they might not even know they had heard.

HOMECOMINGS AND FRIGHTENING HOLIDAYS

"Your dad's coming home this weekend." The mother's hand shook as she lowered the platter of pork chops to the checkered tabletop. "Probably tomorrow night." She wiped her palms against the apron, though her hands were not wet. "He was in Canada when he called. It may take him till Saturday. But he'll be here."

"Did you send him the money to get home?"

The daughter's question alerted Plum immediately to a different tension, a problem different from what she had surmised.

"Why does that matter?"

John had risen from his chair and was turning toward the hallway.

"You sit back down," the mother said. "You're not leaving without eating."

"I'm not hungry."

"You'll eat anyhow." She put a big, deep-blue bowl next to the platter. Steam rose from potatoes whipped so fine they peaked.

John said nothing, but the set of his lips implied no one could push food between them. His fine, small-boned frame had gone rigid. This person was a hostage, but certainly not captured.

"Let him go, Mom," the girl said. "Nobody can eat feeling like John does."

The mother turned her back to them both, carefully draining the green beans of some liquid but keeping the seasoning bits of pork fat. She didn't speak. Plum, peering from behind artificial grapes on the refrigerator, saw tears welling in the woman's eyes, saw them spill over her lower lashes. The mother quickly put down the pan and grabbed a dishtowel, as if only to dry her hands, but instead touched the cloth to her damp cheeks and eyes. She opened a drawer and unfolded a clean white cotton cloth. Then, fortified by the action, she turned and smiled at her children.

"You're right, Catherine. You may go, John. I'll leave the food on the table. When you feel like eating . . ."

He was already out of sight, and the slight hushshsh of a closing door momentarily kept daughter and mother silent.

"I don't know what to do." The woman sat down at the table.

"Don't let him come home."

"I have to, honey. This is his home, too."

"No, it's not." The girl stiffened herself and looked boldly at her mother. "And when he's here, it's not ours either. He doesn't love us."

"Don't say that, Catherine. Please. Don't even think it."

"He doesn't love John, Momma. And he doesn't love me. How can you believe he loves you?" Then, with grace that made Plum's own small heart clench and start again, Catherine pushed her chair properly against the table and walked down the hall. Plum heard the steps pause, heard, "It's okay, John," before they resumed. The mother stared at the kitchen window, opaque now from the steam within and the descending darkness outside.

The child was too wise too soon. The child had become parent.

Plum, unable to disappear at will or to correct such terrible ills at once, sat down behind the grapes and leaned against them. She wept. Somebody had to.

* * *

PLUM PACED THE BRANCH, every turn a danger. "We are going to stay with them every moment."

Crow nodded.

"We will make The Argul stay away. He won't enter this house, not ever." Crow nodded again, not because he agreed with Plum or believed he and she could enforce her desires, but because the little fury needed agreement. The possibility of defeat should not peek over her horizon. A champion must chase away all doubts and spur her onward. A champion.

"CAW!"

THE MOON HAD RISEN dusky gold, as if behind rich silk, and the sky around it was a subdued, burnished dark, as if it might burst into moonlight itself, and flood the entire universe with a new light. A few gray clouds wafted very high, like boats having taken the wrong ocean, so enthralled by a new beauty the travelers did not know they were lost. Between heaven and earth, birds coasted or flew, drawn to enjoy this in-between world. In the streets of small towns, children approached strange doors, strangely decorated. On some steps, residents waited, a bowl or sack of treats in hand, eager to see the costumed young; other couples stayed inside but hastened to answer a light knock or a timid "trick or treat." Parents kept a judicious distance from their smallest children, allowing them freedom to feel however they would —brave, frightened, greedy, happy. All Hallows' Eve. Halloween.

"It's like they're coming from the shadows," Plum said.

"Do I detect fear in your voice? Of children?"

"No, you do not. I may feel some . . . trepidation from shadows—shadows that may not be children, but something else entirely."

"Trepidation."

"It means . . ."

"I know, Mistress Plum, the meaning. Its use at this time is less clear to me."

"Very well, then." She seemed about to chastise him. "Very well, then." A deep, wavery breath. "I'm afraid, Crow, of what stalks these children."

"It's not a shadow, Miss. Nor is it so easily seen."

"No."

They were insecurely positioned at the best vantage point to see all approaches to the house—on the highest limb of a fading pine tree. The branch was not too hardy and quite bare of needles—it was much like a large needle itself—but they could quickly speed in any direction.

"It's foolish of me," Crow's words came to Plum, "but I wish we could give the children treats."

"They will acquire more than enough, I'm sure."

"What if they don't? What if no one gives them any treat of value? I mean one worth having. I mean one other than can be had for a penny or found by the wayside."

Plum had turned her dark eyes upward, trying to grasp what lay behind Crow's words, what was causing the encroaching sadness from the creature most apt to be bragging or brandishing or believing in the best outcome.

"Crow?"

"What!"

"Are you speaking angrily to me? For what reason?"

Silence. Then, "No reason you've earned. But some children—many—are forever disappointed and learn that for themselves, no special treat will ever be forthcoming. Only adequate is their lot and should be enough, one supposes. 'Tis a hard lesson."

Plum, whose tiny being had responded to Crow's words with wild emotion, jumped to her feet. "Well, I am now finished in this conversation," she announced. "I finally get calm, and what do you do? You become a harbinger of doom and damnation. Eee'll hae nooon o'tha. Eee will not. Eee will not." Zip. Plum was gone. Not disappeared. Just flying down slowly, like a purple leaf that was unusually thickly ruffled, with a white under-flounce not often, if ever, seen. Had she ever received less than she longed for? Had she been a privileged child? Spoiled?

Crow, uncertain of the source of his deep concern, zipped away, too, but in a different direction—to the main street of the tiny town. He alighted on the tar roof of Mechan's Five and Dime. With a few upward thrusts and sideways tugs of his sturdy beak he dislodged the rain cap plug on the attic vent and, though he disliked putting his head into a pipe leading down, where flight might not be possible, he did not hesitate. He ran, actually, forward. Brave Crow. His claws against the thin metal scratched a high shriek that some night creatures heard—their eyes widened. If they had tails, the tails perked. So did ears. Eeeek. They passed on this warning of an unknown high-voiced threat. Zoom to safety; peek out; listen. Special night; special fright. One foolhardy squirrel stayed right where he was, eyes big as ancient coins, but lustrous. He had seen a dashing crow and wanted to see it again. The squirrel was not at all certain he himself was meant to be a squirrel. Perhaps a crow? At least friends with one.

Inside the closed Five and Dime, Crow walked along the candy bins, eyeing the hard nuggets that would make small mouths work too hard for too little sweetness. He spurned such treats. He flew down the aisles. Then, understanding that what had value to humans would be kept under close watch, he flew to the register counter. And there, where managers could guard their profits, were bins of chocolate. Wrapped chocolate. Clean and neat. Crow got in each bin, careful not to puncture wrapping. His sensitive claws felt for the freshest candy, and he made a good-sized stack of those pieces. On another quick scouting, he found a packaged red handkerchief, tore off the cardboard circlet, shook out the handkerchief, placed the candy on it, and, after some struggling and mild explosions of air that might have been gentle curses, had a bag of candy that would withstand dangling from the beak of a soaring master of the skies.

Now, how to get out? He couldn't get even himself up the attic vent pipe. He would slide back. He surveyed the large room, high ceiling. Above the entryway a display window jutted toward the street, protected by an eave. Below the point of the eave was a hole where something had fallen out or been removed, and a piece of oil cloth now hung limply, held only by a sole remaining tack. In one long swoop down, Crow had the bag, and arced back. By clinging with one claw to the edge of the hole, and the handkerchief corners clamped in his beak, he pushed the candy bag through from the bottom, in bits, till only he and the corners were inside the store. Out! Up!

Down the streaked sky above Prairie Street, alighting on the hedge by the front walk. When Catherine and John emerged, each holding a paper bag with cut-out smiles bordering the top, Crow realized he needed *two* bags. Was one's work never done? As the children reached the true sidewalk, Crow hopped down, forward, and deposited the red-bagged plunder before them, an equal distance from each. Then he was off. Oooh. Such wonder. Such joy. To give sweet treats. To this girl and boy.

Inside the Five and Dime again, Crow would have sung except that crows cannot do so. His varied softer sounds, clicks, rattles, and soft grunts, filled the front of the store where he again deposited a hill of candy onto a red handkerchief. With this wrapped, and secure in beak, he rushed to Paul's. Paul was still there but surrounded by the boys who had accompanied him at the river. They were in costumes. Not Paul. Nor did he have a bag for sweets.

Crow assessed them, the bag still in his mouth.

"I got some soap," one said.

"Got four eggs," from another.

"Raw hamburger meat!"

Aspiring little demons. Crow darted forward, landing on Paul's shoulder, though facing the wrong way. He turned quickly. The handkerchief swung down past Paul's collarbone. Crow could smell the chocolate and assumed his friend could, too.

Crow could also smell hamburger but refused to let its appeal be obvious to anyone. The egg boy locked his vision on Paul for moments, then ran straightaway to the west. The other boys moved uneasily, not quite as close to Paul as they had been. Above them all the orange moon seemed wider, closer.

A sound like "Gar!" blurted from the soap boy's lips.

Paul took the handkerchief. "I trained him. You know, like a carrier pigeon."

Crow contorted himself enough to lightly peck his friend's earlobe. It was pretend punishment for a lie that was well warranted and wittily executed.

Finding a spot where the moonlight made the bag's contents visible, Paul knelt and counted out the pieces of candy. He gave each remaining boy an equal share. The last two he returned to the handkerchief and deposited in his pocket.

Was he, then, taking two for himself? Like the master warrior's share? Crow waited.

"I'll give Tom his tomorrow," Paul said.

Crow stretched up with pride. His boy!

Paul stood. "You guys still want to go trick-or-treating?"

They did. They moved off. If they had been on a ship, Crow would have been in the crow's nest, the loftiest perch, to serve as lookout for his fellows.

"Caw!"

The boys mimicked the sound—a little flock of ne'er-do-wells out for adventure.

Crow attempted a laugh of pleasure, and the boys echoed that lighter Caw!

Crow positioned himself to fly where the scent of hamburger, agonizingly tempting, was strongest. Plum, he suspected, would have raged.

PLUM HAD BEEN DIRECTLY behind her charges when Crow dropped his bag of sweets at their feet. His generous and dramatic act had pleased her, and in her amusement she missed the immediate reaction of the girl, Catherine. When Plum did hear her concern, it was expressed in a calm, determined voice. "It had to be from a devil, because that was a blackbird."

"A crow, specifically," John said. "There's lots of blackbirds, and birds who are black in color. But this is a crow."

"Crows work for the devil, too."

"No, they don't." He walked as steadily as he spoke.

"Crows are birds. They don't work for anybody but themselves unless they want to or are forced to."

"They're a sign of death. You ask Momma."

John didn't answer. When their words neared the topic of
parents, the children became cautious, quiet—and sometimes
even mute.

Viewed from behind, the children could have been waifs
running away. Even in costumes, they were both very slender, and though this was apparently a family trait, and
though they were well fed as far as Plum had determined, the
thinness made them appear fragile, as if they hadn't yet taken
shape and might, as they walked into the Halloween night,
fade into the shadows and never return.

Plum had frightened herself with her own thoughts and
sped up, flying now with her hands behind her back. It was,
to someone else who viewed her, such as a sharp-eyed squirrel, an interesting position. The squirrel had seen a ribbon
once, and Plum appeared like a live ribbon, floating in a
zigzagging, purple stream above two human children.
Squirrel followed, running from tree trunk to tree trunk,
head up, tail flicking, sniffing, run, run. Sit, sniff. Adventure.

Plum's children met other children, and the sidewalks
glowed not from light but from the pleasant exchanges and
teasings of young voices on a holiday evening. They were
happy to pretend not to know one another, to squeal
surprise when a mask was removed, or a name whispered.
Pretense and playful lying were part of the celebration. So
was indulgence. Plum felt sorry for the few children whose
parents said, "Nothing now. You may have one piece when
we get home. The rest you'll save."

Save? Save? Save pleasure like a penny? Have it turn dull
and useless and all its possible beauty fade forever, not
regainable? Gone. Plum herself would have eaten fifteen
hundred thousand pieces to make life more wonderful for all

children. "A million," she exclaimed. She knew, though, that she had no time to taste even one bit now. Duty first. She was, after all, no child. Regrettably. Most regrettably.

Her charges and a few other children had moved south down Prairie Street, toward the huge courthouse from whose dome a clock face shone in all directions. Four clocks, really, each with a different time, and all those times wrong, Plum supposed. She wondered, though, if the four clocks were wrong, what if all time everywhere were wrong. What if there were no time at all?

Now she had frightened herself again. She attended the children.

At the courthouse, the children by custom walked around it, to face the direction from which they had come and then head home. They would pass children going the opposite way, so it was like a carousel with steeds running in counter-circles.

"This is a magic walk," Catherine said to John. "Just on Halloween Night."

"There's no such thing."

"Yes, there is. And it's also magic at twelve midnight. At the witching hour."

When John didn't respond, Catherine said, "That crow was a witch's familiar."

"A what?"

Catherine stopped as if she'd tell him, she most certainly would, but the shadow of a quick-flitting thing fell across her brother's face. It didn't frighten her. In fact, it reassured her. John was a small boy. Her brother. Hers.

"Nothing," Catherine said. She reached for his hand. "Let's go home."

John hesitated but he didn't take her hand. "I'm okay," he said.

They headed around the curve to the South Prairie side

and encountered Paul and his friends sitting across the sidewalk, blocking access to either side. Names had been written in soap across the concrete, and the waxy streaks glowed unevenly.

"Five pieces of candy if you want to get by us," one boy said. He stood, reached for John's bag. "And we get to pick them."

John put the bag behind his back.

Catherine, who was very lovely in the moonlight, tugged John's shirt sleeve. "Come on, John. Let's go the other way."

John resisted, pulled free. He was a strawman and pieces of straw jutted from his shirt collar and cuffs. For shoes, he wore large socks stuffed with straw. On his head, shadowing his gentle features, was an old straw hat, punched to cone-shape, and circled with a strip of red velvet. Red, the color of bravery and often the cost of victory. So thought Plum and Catherine about John, though the words might change with each speaker and with each age.

Catherine stayed right beside him. She was dressed in a sheet draped like a toga, which she believed was the attire of Greek warriors. She resembled most, though, a young maiden who desired and merited a sash of silk instead of a length of rope, and who should have, perhaps, a flower circlet woven into her hair.

So thought the young boys and Crow about Catherine, though they might not know the words or history to express their knowledge.

"Five pieces," the same boy said, "and that's if you count them out. If we got to do it, then there's no counting at all. We get the bag." The voice was more stuttery than tough, even to the speaker himself. "Cough it up."

At that moment Crow descended in a shaft of moonlight not on Paul's shoulder where he had first planned to light, but on John's much lower shoulder. And there, on the brim of the hat, crowning the exact same child, was a purple-gowned, minute vision, Plum, like a queen reduced to memory and suggestion.

First was a silence so profound the universe itself might have been holding its breath, and there was such glory in the moment, moonlight and choice.

"No," said John, and Catherine, though still astonished at the black symbol sitting on her brother's shoulder, said "no" so closely the two sounds blended in one word.

Though the soap boy had seemed forceful only a moment before, he now hesitated. No one rallied to his side.

Paul got to his feet but stayed close to his group of would-be-bullies. "Leave them alone," he said, indicating that Catherine and John should be troubled no more. He nodded briefly, almost a shallow bow, toward the brother and sister. He turned his back to them all. "I'm going home," came his surprisingly firm voice. "I'm too old for Halloween anyway."

John continued standing where he was.

"Let's go," Catherine said.

John, for whom silence was often a response, waited a few seconds more, as if a decision were being made. Then he stepped forward and set his bag of treats down with contempt, or as much of that attitude as a young boy dressed in straw and rags may convey. "For you little kids," he said, and turned his back on the candy. Two forms flitted up, toward the moon. Child gasps were lost in the sudden, erroneous, but deep and somber sounding of the clock chime.

Catherine, eyes proud and flashing, had turned with John, but had been unable to relinquish her own treasure of candy. If they didn't walk in unison with the massive chimes, they seemed to. It etched a perfect memory in her heart. She wanted to say, "I love you, John," but she couldn't. Such words couldn't be said in certain moments. One simply felt them, endured them. Oh, she loved her brother.

And oh, Crow and Plum loved them all.

With the best part of the best Halloween over, they ambled home, John and Catherine on foot, and Crow and Plum on wing and wish above them. Children still appeared, but there were fewer and they seemed more daring than childlike, as if they were older but not yet willing to take the step that cost one more holiday belief.

"I want to know why that bird got on *your* shoulder." Catherine looked sideways at her brother. "You hear me? He jumped right onto you, John, like he was your bird."

"He's a crow."

"That's a bird."

Silence from her newest hero. "A crow," Catherine said. "What was that thing with him?"

"I don't know."

That was not true, and Catherine knew it. She stopped walking, tilted her head back and looked straight up. The act made her dizzy but the reward was to see two spirals unable to disappear fast enough, one quite large, the other very small.

"You're a witch," she said. "We're in the hands of the devil."

They walked on, a little more rapidly.

"Warlock," she corrected.

"What?" from John.

"A male witch. Warlock."

In a moment, John sped up. A few seconds later, he and Catherine were each attempting not to be the one to break into a run.

The shadows were fatter now, one merging into the other, as if night were not something that descended or fell, but that spread, wrapping over and around, slipping under and up. Down the tilting sidewalk, stepping over the raised, wide cracks, down the street to North Prairie.

A streetlight had been shattered. Shards of glass crossed the road like a dare-line in the waning moon. Somewhere behind them were footsteps. Or echoes of footsteps. Who could tell when hearts raced and breath came short?

"What's that?" from Catherine.

"I don't know. Let's run."

So they did. Behind them, Paul, who had trailed them only to assure that no one from his gang pulled any shameful stunts, sped up, too, and not just to keep pace. No one wants to be alone when night settles over a small town, when streetlights have been blackened, when doors are locked. The person left outside would feel as if he or she or they were the only beings alive in the world.

A young squirrel was feeling just that.

Plum was feeling edgy. "I almost know something," she said.

Crow knew what she meant but had first to say, "All creatures are in that state— almost knowing something."

Plum made no sharp retort, though she was very capable of doing so. She was concentrating on the foreboding overcoming her. "Something's amiss," she said.

Crow let that opportunity pass. He dashed forward and down the peak of their family's roof. And immediately he knew. "The Argul has come," he thought.

Plum floated down slowly, coming to rest on his strong back, between the beginning arch of wing bones. "Yes. He's inside."

"Yes."

"And here come the children."

"Yes. Here come the children."

A MEETING IN TIME

"They know The Argul's home," Plum said, shifting her gaze from the two children to Crow.

"Yes. 'Tis sad."

Plum sighed. "I must follow them in." She slid down to the roof peak beside him.

"I, too."

Both knew the proper response: No. Crow was not small enough or quiet enough. He could cause more harm than good, even if the harm were no more than fear or consternation.

"Birds in the house are disturbing to some humans," Crow acknowledged.

"Only blackbirds."

"You do mean black birds? All of them? You are speaking of color and not species?"

"It won't work, Crow. You may not lighten this moment for either of us."

She was gone, so quickly Crow thought perhaps she hadn't flown at all but blinked away. Then he saw the fast-beating hover, Plum, not far from the young girl's hair. He lost sight of the children when they stepped onto the porch, concealed by the roof. He swooped down, lighting first on hedge, then on rosebush outside a lighted window, on back stoop, and finally on the lowest branch of the pecan tree, from where he could see the yellow square of kitchen behind glass. This way and that he turned his fine head, as if to conjure the humans up where he could see them. He retraced his path around the house, looking for one clear view, listening for a coherent spoken phrase. Where were the children? Where was Plum? Then back, flapping wildly to the pecan tree, leaning down. Listen! Listen!

"Oh Crow," he heard as a thought in sweet Plum's voice. "The mother's telling him he'll have to leave. She's crying. The children can hear it all! And The Argul is angry, very angry! Crow. Crow. Crow."

This was maddening. He was a cumbersome clod, a fumbling fool. Down to the dark ground and the dead grass, scurrying forward. Where was the entrance? Where had Plum fashioned her own pathway? "Caw! Caw! I'm coming, I'm coming. Eee'mm ahn mee wae!"

Just as he found the corner of the crawlspace door, another movement caught him and around he spun, looking for what it was. By the edge, somewhere near the deepest part of the yard, before the ditch, to the right of their tree.

A muted, dull, kind of screech jerked his attention back. A squirrel was at the crawlspace entrance, clinging upside down on the house shingles and tugging up the hook. Then he flicked his tail and was a few shingles up, turning upside down again to give Crow a fervid and wild look. Crow had never been stared at so directly by a squirrel. He believed the creature to be insane. But the door was open and Crow ran across the dirt floor, listening and searching for the tiny space upward, into the . . . what? What was it? The flue. What did a flue look like? He must find the opening Plum used, any opening. He scurried through the darkness, seeking a flicker from upstairs, a way in. Alarmed by a sense of danger outside, too, he glanced at the crawlspace entrance. There was the damnable squirrel, hanging upside down, agitated, looking not at Crow, but into the moonlit yard. Crow didn't know where the true battle was, where he was needed. He waited, torn, heart and mind fast but unable to act because he simply did not yet know enough. "Plum," he thought, and tried to listen closer than ever he had.

Inside the house, Plum was very near Catherine. The young girl had sunk into a deep blue chair in her bedroom. Her legs were drawn up beside her, as if she'd curl into the chair itself, and not be a young girl trembling from a man's raging and a woman's crying. Just above her braids, on a carved wood-curl in the side-wing of the chair, sat Plum. All the sounds of this particular moment came to her like discordant music, so that she heard Crow beneath the house, heard his new companion's chittering warning, heard the boy in his room, and, superseding them all, the voices filling the kitchen. No longer was that room the soft center of the house, but a hard and brittle place, where now threatened a split of the children's world.

The Argul was defending himself. "I do the best I can. It's not like I have a choice of jobs, you know. I work hard. Those engineers, they think they can boot me around just because I can't pass the exam. I know more than they do. You know what it's like? Taking orders from a man who knows less than you do? I'm the one that keeps the barge going. The boat's engine is mine! I've repaired it so much I've built it from scratch. We've never missed a deadline on my run."

"I'm talking about us," the woman said. "Not the river. Not the men. We have kids and they have troubles, too. They need things. Clothes. We need a car."

"You don't need a car. You don't go anywhere."

"I work. I walk to that blessed factory every morning, no matter the weather. And I carry groceries home. There's nobody to help me. Or these kids. I can't do it all, Argul. I'm tired. What if another baby comes along? I can't take any more."

"What are you telling me?"

"You're a different man when you're drinking. I'm telling you we get scared when you do come home. We dread it."

"We?"

"The kids and I."

"You're making that up. Catherine is crazy about me."

"So's Johnny. But neither of them wants you here."

"I don't believe it. You just want to hurt me."

The mother's words were stuttered, broken by light sobbing. "That, too. I do want to hurt you, Argul, like you hurt me, all the time, so I'd rather be dead."

Beside Plum, the young girl gasped.

Oh! Parents should be flogged. They should have to live half a world away from children until the parents grew up. How dare they speak such words where children could hear? Where young hearts could be broken or hardened in self-defense. Who could Plum fight? Who could she defeat? She had to protect one of the children. Both if possible.

Crow!

Sounds of a chair being moved came from the kitchen, followed by the ominous, heavy tread of The Argul coming up the sloping hall. Catherine drew tense, rigid, as she did at night before exhaustion brought her sleep. She pressed her right index knuckle to her lips and stared at the heavy green curtains serving as bedroom door. The footsteps stopped for seconds and Plum knew he stood outside the boy's door. But then the steps resumed. Into the living room. Across it. The green curtains were parting.

Catherine had put her feet on the floor and sat forward.

"Hey, kid!" The words were obviously meant to be light-hearted.

"I'm not a kid."

"You're my kid. My girl." He moved very cautiously, smiling in an unpleasant, lopsided way. He sat on a trunk at the foot of the bed, facing Catherine in the chair. He lighted a cigarette, puffed at it though the fire had caught immediately. Thick and wavery columns of smoke rose upward. A dresser mirror reflected his back as a dark hump, his head crowned with black curly hair. There, he appeared a different man, misshapen, nobody's father, perhaps not even human.

"How you doing?"

The girl shrugged, looked away.

"Your mom says you don't want me to live here."

No answer.

"Is that right?"

She shrugged again.

"You can talk, can't you? Your mom can sure say enough."

"Don't talk about Mom."

"Oh. She's been getting to you."

"Don't talk about her, that's all."

He leaned his head back, exhaled smoke.

Plum herself felt frightened. She thought quickly, solemnly, to the girl. "Thee est most fine, most lovely. Thee needn't speak to this creature, nor meet his eyes. Hold thy ground."

The Argul spoke. "This is my house, too, you know. My name's on the paper. Your mom couldn't buy it without me."

Catherine, though she seemed near to exploding from the room, repeatedly rubbed her left thumb into the opposite palm. The action was, perhaps, to calm herself.

Plum, though not letting her guard down, could see beauty in The Argul, as perhaps Catherine and the mother saw him. He had wide-spaced eyes, silky curls, white skin, a firm mouth and jaw. His eyes were moist, as if he might cry. Plum was astonished. What was this?

"Mom paid for it," Catherine said. Now she rubbed her palms against her knees, as if her hands sweated. The room, though, was cool, almost cold.

"I make real good money on the river."

"Mom pays for everything." On the last word, her voice rose, insistent. Then she repeated, "Everything."

Something was amiss here. Something was supposed to occur or was occurring and Plum didn't know what it was. She looked from The Argul to Catherine, again and again, hoping to divine.

Then the sheer femininity of Catherine became so evident that Plum sighed with understanding. She noted the delicate turn of the girl's wrists, the tilt of her young and pretty head, the now gracefully crossed ankles. Plum touched her fingertips to her lips. Of course. The daughter of a handsome man, of a gadabout, a romantic ne'er-do-well. The child Catherine had adored him. But on the brink of adulthood, Catherine sees the twice-abandoned brother, the over-burdened mother, and she pleads as an adult for her father to value them. He fails. And thus she fails, as daughter, sister, and young woman. She had a final hope. Now she has to choose when the heart doesn't want to.

Words were not enough; alone, Plum couldn't change their lives. Catherine was filling with emotion that could be love or hate, with longing and resistance that were apt to bring action before maturity and thrust her into an unhappy, angry world. Plum said, aloud, "Love each other!" and though her words weren't understood, and even the direction of the movement and sound wasn't clear, the two people in her vision responded to action with action—it was the wrong action, but to remain the same was impossible.

Catherine jumped up. "I hate you." She clenched her small

hands, held them so tightly they shook. "I wish you were dead. If John doesn't kill you, *I* will. *I* will. I will take a lamp and hit you in the head." She was crying. Her face contorted, and so did Plum's, her feelings so wrapped up in the child she could not separate herself momentarily and felt that she, too, was saying she hated him and would kill him. She was appalled at herself. Stricken dumb. The child fled. The curtains, parted for her escaping form, fell into place. The man stared at them, then at the floor. He sat back, though the movement was involuntary, much like falling. With elbows on knees, hands clasped, he could have been attempting a prayer, though Plum knew that wasn't his action. He was lost, momentarily at least, and perhaps for longer. "I'll be damned," he whispered. "The kid hates me. My own kid." He looked directly at Plum but did not see her. He was, Plum hoped, looking inside himself.

Moments later, he stood and pushed through the curtains. "John!" He headed toward the boy's room.

"No." Plum followed. "No."

He pushed at the door but it caught. "Unlock the door," he said. "John."

His wife was in the hallway, framed by the kitchen light. "Leave him alone, Argul."

"Open the door, John. I just want to talk. Open it. Open it! I'll kick it down, so help me . . ."

He kicked.

Plum darted, spun, arced up.

The Argul was coming into the room. John was in the center of the bed, crying. The rifle was aimed at his stepfather.

"No!" Plum thought and said and acted. She threw herself between the two.

Outside, the gold moon outlined the house, yard, the running form of a young girl. She dropped to her knees and sobbed. From near the house a huge shadow emerged. It hunched close to the side hedge but moved steadily toward the girl. Beneath the house, a trembling but ever so quiet Crow took awkward, clutching, claw-steps toward the crawlspace exit. He was in agony from the battle above, which he felt throughout his brave, dark being. But he stayed on course, toward the backyard, guided and encouraged by the furry, flicking creature hanging upside down on the crawlspace door, breathing fast, marking seconds. Squirrel.

"Argul!" the woman screamed in the hallway. "John! Please, for the love of God."

Another scream came from outside. "Daddy!"

Argul burst into the hallway, down it, down the steps to the low back room, out the door. He fell down those steps and, pushing up, heard not screaming, but deeper sounds, like thuds, grunts, and coarse bird sounds, "Cawraush, Cawraush." And? Something else. He ran, like a maddened and terrified creature, and came to an abrupt stop near the clothesline. Someone had Catherine! The man's hand was pressed over her white face, covering her features. No sound came from her. But the man was staggering. One arm came up to protect himself from a feathered vengeance that was unstoppable. He had to release the girl or be blinded. He turned to run. A small creature had clenched to his back and was at the side of his throat.

The man cursed, a loud stream like dark oil coming up from the earth.

Argul ran to his daughter who lay limply on the cool ground. "Catherine. Kid. Baby. Catherine." He glanced only once at the running form. He slipped his arms beneath his daughter and lifted her gently.

Yes, Plum thought. The child first. Always the child first.

Just as he straightened, he saw his wife standing frozen with fear.

"She's okay," he said. "She'll be okay."

Plum, suspended in moonlight, watched until the parents had closed the back door. Then she zoomed around the house, alighting at Crow's side on the porch swing.

Before them, the huge monster sat in the very middle of the family's walkway. He was the one who had watched young Catherine as she tried to undo freckles with moonlight; he was the one who had rolled out of the back seat of the car, looking for Argul. Now, he was subdued! He was so thick-necked and heavy bodied that he could neither draw his fat legs up nor lay them flat. He couldn't sit erect but leaned backwards and propped himself steady with stiff arms, palms on the concrete walk. Plum was pleased at his discomfort. Betrayer of friendships and humanity. Suffer.

A few feet from him was the young man Paul, most definitely a young man, not a boy, who held a heavy piece of lumber as though it were a baseball bat. On the porch step, tiny but sitting very erect and alert, was John, rifle pointed at the man.

"I wish I had seen this," Plum said.

"Nothing unpleasant is pleasant to see," Crow responded.

"Justice is."

"Justice is not visible. Pain is, right or wrong."

"Do you think so? Just the other night you attacked this very . . ."

The front door opened. Argul emerged, still not steadily. "I'll be right back," he said. "I'll get the doctor." He saw the inhabitants of his front yard. "What the . . ."

"I'll call the doctor, sir," Paul said. "Our neighbor has a phone. I can get the sheriff, too."

"You do that." He seemed uncertain what he should do, where he should go. He sat down heavily by John. "I'll stay with my boy here."

John scooted away.

Argul took out a cigarette, but he did not light it. From the monster on the walkway came whining words. "Why don't you let me go home, Argul? I was just teasing the kids a little, trying to give them a Halloween scare. After all, no real harm done."

Argul didn't answer. In a moment he said to John, "You hold that rifle a lot steadier than I could. At least, than I could right now. You keep it on him."

"I don't need your help," John said. Again, he moved just enough to show what he felt. Alone.

"I only went after you to talk. I wouldn't hurt you."

Behind them, the mother stood in the open, lighted doorway. Her shadow fell between them.

"I could use some coffee," Argul said.

"No. Not here. Not now."

Argul glanced at his former buddy, ducked his head briefly, and turned to face his wife. "I understand. I'll stay out here or go away. Whatever you want. I'm sorry. Tell Catherine I'm sorry. Nothing like this will ever happen again." He looked at John. "I'm sorry to you, too, and your friend." John didn't acknowledge him. Argul rose, moved unsteadily to the swing.

Plum was again very weary. But being next to Crow, feeling the warmth radiate from his energetic, protective self, was very comforting. Occasionally he twisted around to look at the tree near the walk, and each time Plum's gaze followed his. There, on a low branch was a nervous, almost frantic happiness with a furry tail who would run a foot or so down the limb, squeak at the man on the walk, then retreat.

"He thinks he's a crow," Crow said.

"How do you know?"

"Don't ask me. Some answers come without my asking a question."

"I know."

"I thought you did."

"Maybe he just wants to be a crow but knows he's a squirrel."

"Maybe. But he's the one gave me the signal to emerge."

"And what then? What did I miss?"

"A fine boy in a fine moment. Paul was in the front yard. I saw him swing a board, a solid, broad, hefty, mighty weapon, and it bent the monster double and brought him down. Then John appeared with rifle in hand. He sat down on the porch. With one boy standing and one sitting, that creature," he nodded toward the huge man, "has been immobilized. It was worthy work and well done."

"And Crow is most happy."

He nodded again, deeply, like a bow. "Most."

LATE IN THE NIGHT, Plum woke. Without alerting Crow, though he most certainly knew anyhow, she stole into the house, to look at the girl, Catherine. Peace was not yet there. The girl's features were drawn tight, even in sleep. Plum wanted to help more. She tried whispering the father's name, "Argul," so the daughter would know that she had that parent's love, too. But Plum couldn't do it. Had he earned such help? No. What had he done but cause pain? No help would come from her. Let him learn to express himself in good ways or remain mute. She lay down on the pillow alongside her young charge and fell almost into sleep herself. Would she ever find her own father? Even in memory? In dream? Was he handsome? One night or day she would slip up on that knowledge like a treasure and own it forever. Not now, though. Now came other duties, came whatever had caused her to waken into a life where she was only two-inches tall, was accompanied by a loving, but too-challenging Crow. She stretched and yawned. The movement altered her field of vision. There was the picture frame, white, on the wall above the bed. A white square in the filmy room, holding a picture she had seen each night when she entered the room, but rarely thought of.

Plum stood, then flew up, hovering right before the picture. That angel, that blonde, unbelievable, gigantic creature. Each of the white slender hands was over the head of a child, as if protecting. The angel's gown was white, the children were plump, dressed in rich clothing. Something was amiss there, too, but Plum could not bring herself to quarrel with the appearance of an angel or the execution of its duties. Still, unable to constrain her feelings entirely, she struck lightly her own chest, as if proclaiming either contest or conquest. Wasn't she a protector, too, or learning how to be? Immediately, afire with spirit, she flew back to the pillow, placed five kisses on each cheek of the dear, upturned face, and with a hasty glance at the picture, zoomed out of the room, down the hall, to the flue, under the house, and to her tree.

"It is easier to rest," she heard upon landing, "if one stops flitting about."

"One may rest while the other may flit." With a flounce, she entered her rooms and lay down fully clothed. She closed her eyes, fell into sleep.

And dreamed. She ran weeping into a vast garden of blossoms and small fruit trees. She could find no place for comfort, nothing to still her tears or lessen the ache of her heart. He was gone. She would never see him again. She had too often been haughty! Oh, she wished herself small, away from the horrid world of adults who took all the beauty from life in the name of proper and fitting, away from pain and sorrow. She threw herself down and petals fell around and over her. Surely he would seek her again. Hearts must find a way.

When Crow was certain Plum slept, he, too, flew to the little house. He found Argul still on the porch swing, restlessly sleeping. Crow alighted on the swing's top slat and eyed the man a while, listened to his uneven breathing, small cries and moans. Were they from drunkenness or pain? How could Crow address such a nature, an adult man who was thoughtless, selfish, even mean? Was Argul burdened with an illness that stole will? Crow had no memories of someone like this, no experience, no comforting words or thoughts. He hopped on the man's shoulder and began a low rumble that smoothed into a hum. He hummed while he thought of peacefully gliding through shafts of moonlight, round and round, up and down. When the hum ended, Crow sat in silence. Then he nudged the man's cheek with the rounded and blunt tip of his beak and flew with slow flaps over the backyard to the tree and Plum.

In the morning, Plum woke to vague memories of unhappiness. She studied her gown. It was still purple brocade, not quite so full, not silk, coarser, with a high, double-layered bodice. Suitable for the new season. From the center of the bed, she stretched out her arms, palms up. "Come!"

The dress did not move. She stood, an uneasy pose on the soft mattress. She extended her arms again, but up, as if raising them for a dress to be lowered over her.

"Be *on* me, then."

Nothing.

"Robe me!"

Nothing.

She stomped to the edge of her bed, leapt down, and snapped the gown from the briar hook.

"What if I wanted pants? What if I wanted an apron? What if I wanted a crown?"

A handsome bird's face filled her arched doorway. "What

if I wanted a different companion? One who did not have unseemly tantrums at early hours."

"This is no tantrum. This is command."

"Perhaps you need to learn request."

"A lady dresses."

"A Crow withdraws."

When she had her winter gown on, and had piled her black curls high, to be as tall as possible, she strolled out onto their branch. "We did a fine deed."

"We helped."

"But we are not quite finished with them?"

"No." Crow pushed a dried leaf with up-curved sides toward her. On it were bits of crust, as if pinched from the side of a pie, each covered with pumpkin.

"Pumpkin pie! My favorite!"

"How would you know?"

Plum sighed. Not just pie, but sweet potatoes, the tiny cut edges of ham, where a rind had been removed, the soft top corner of a biscuit, a suspiciously pointed peak of butter.

"I can never, of course, provide turkey for you," Crow thought to her. "Though I might eat it myself."

"I understand."

"One's own, in a manner of speaking."

"A most gracious manner. Will you join me?"

Crow did so, eating delicately the portions Plum divided and slid to him.

"The Argul," she said, "may not drink today."

"Perhaps not." Crow ate a sliver of ham. "But then again, he may."

"He should leave," Plum announced. Her nod was firm. "He makes their life much harder."

"Good judgment is a fine virtue in a rash creature; rash judgment a dangerous vice in a good creature."

"My word, Crow!"

"Mine, I believe, and more than one."

They laughed, but Crow's eyes had a somber cast. Plum squirmed, as if her perch on the limb were uncomfortable. Then she relinquished a bit of pride. "Am I, then, judging again? Wrongly?"

"You would help those you find endearing and toss away the one they love."

"Oh!" she jumped up. "You maddening creature. Are you never, ever, through chastising me?"

"I'm not chastising."

"You are! You are! And I'll not have it."

"When I'm ashamed of your behavior—though never of you—I must say so." Crow turned his back on her. She stared at the fine feathers, how their luster ran together like a soft but impenetrable shield. Before her was the table he had prepared. Not for himself. He had brought her the nourishment she needed. She understood that Crow's nature was his own, as hers was hers.

And The Argul's?

Must she tell *him*, too, that he was loved? Was that the next duty?

"Perhaps the final one," she heard, Crow's response. "And perhaps more pleasure than duty. Once one begins, that is. Action is often much sweeter than thought. He needs to be reminded of responsibility, possible loss of all he loves but abuses. He may need to experience loss."

She resumed her meal, lightly, as yet unable to taste the food.

Crow turned, stepped nearer, and resumed his dignified stance near her. The neighborhood awakened. Wisps of smoke wafted up from the little house and music drifted through a window being opened only a few inches. Chimes sounded from somewhere nearby, and Plum shook her head. Familiar notes. What is the rest of that song? *A circle round, a circle round, a circle round must be.* Must be what?

They heard the approach of someone from farther down the street. Paul appeared—the bully, who had transformed from captor to savior. Broad-shouldered, graceful, he carried a slender pole longer than himself. A fishing rod. He disappeared into the children's front yard and in moments emerged, heading home.

They sped toward the street, Plum turning toward the house and the porch light, to wait on the rod's discovery, and Crow, in slow, rowing fashion, following Paul home. Plum, when the door bolt was thrown, knew without seeing that it was Catherine looking out. How did she know? A scent of perfume or a sense of loneliness? Catherine pushed the screen door out slowly, scanning the yard as she emerged, then looking at the rod for a long moment. "John!" she called, whirling around and back into the house. "John, come quick." Plum wanted to yell, too, and to zoom down and be in that burst of surprise. But it wasn't hers! The moment belonged to John. He followed his sister stoically. He stood over the rod as had Catherine and swept his eyes over it. He picked it up and stepped into the yard before he raised it to test the throw, doing so gently, without loosening the line and without snapping the tip.

"Paul brought it, I'll bet," Catherine said. "Had to be Paul."

John nodded, eyes still on the rod, the handle, the reel, the tip. He lowered it. "I'll put it in my room."

"Aren't you going to thank him?"

"After I have breakfast."

Catherine opened the door for him and he carried the rod horizontally, tucked under one elbow at the middle and guided with the other hand.

"I want to go with you," Catherine said, right behind him.

"Okay." He had to back into his room to angle the rod

inside. He put it beneath his bed and rejoined Catherine. "You can come, but you can't listen. You can't come close."

In the kitchen, blue plates held scrambled eggs, bacon, and toast. Three places were set. The mother was removing her apron. From a radio in a corner of the counter, a song floated through the warm room.

"I guess Paul left that rod," the mother said. "No one else knew about it."

"Did you put it there?" John asked, obviously ready to know the truth, dear brown face, steady brown eyes, strong little fellow.

"I did not. I promise."

With the serving spoon, John scooped eggs into his plate, then pinched two pieces of bacon with his fingers, licking their tips.

"John!" his mother said.

He laughed. Plum did too, just from the sound of his voice and the day.

CROW HAD ANNOUNCED his presence with one CAW and Paul had veered toward the crumbling shed near his house. "Will you wait for me here? Please?" He pushed the half-hinged door inward, waiting for Crow to fly inside, and leaving the door open.

Crow waited on the metal rim of a folded cot and surveyed the surroundings. The boy's special place, his and his friends. Cigarette butts were on a broken plate and in jar lids. Wind whistled and creaked through cracks and open spaces between roof and walls. A wheelbarrow held a mess of tools, rolled plastic cloths, and paint brushes. Paint cans were stacked in a corner, streaked with dried paint. Two ladders lay side by side against a wall. An old sewing machine dangled from its wooden, legged case. Hard times had come and industry had ceased. Help needed here.

Paul entered, holding a big tablet in one hand and a small rectangular bag in the other. "You waited. Thanks." His features showed amazement and happiness. He gestured toward a big wooden spool, turned on its side. "Would you stand on that for a little while?" He raised the tablet. "I want to draw you."

"CAW." Without moving, though Crow was willing if the reason were true.

"You don't want to do it?"

"CAW."

Opening the tablet, Paul approached the folding bed. "See?"

On that page was an image of Plum, very good, but not as small as she was—larger, shaded like a creature coming into being from mist. One of Crow, not as large as he really was, but well presented, erect posture, sleek, soft feathers, black but bright eyes. Other sketches, incomplete, leading to the better ones.

Paul turned the page. Another of Crow and of Plum, still shades of gray and black, but closer to their true size. Around them, faces—his friends. John. A rifle.

Crow stretched his head toward the tablet, gave a gentler response: "Caw"—turn again.

Paul obeyed. Catherine's face. Shades of lovely.

Crow flew into a spot of sunlight on the spool table top. The source of light he didn't know, though he could discover later. Now he was going to be still in this warm place, and let this boy draw him. Paul needed more than pencil and paper.

PLUM AND CROW met at the plum tree, exchanged stories.

Plum exclaimed, "They will be friends! You think, Crow? Yes? Friends?"

"Yes. They need each other. The three, John, Paul, and Catherine."

From feet above came a brief, scattered chittering. A pecan bounced close to Crow, then fell.

"Squirrel has taken to throwing things for our attention," Crow said.

"So I see."

"But he has atrocious aim and less control."

"He needs a cause," Plum said.

"Yes. He may have chosen me."

Plum searched the branches a brief space above and saw the befuddled, hopeful, sparkling, wily eyes of an ardent squirrel. She blew him a kiss.

"Now," Crow thought, "we will never be rid of him."

"As you did not want to be anyway."

"He might have a quest that includes us."

"Oh." Plum sat beside him. "I don't know how I got out of the house," she said. "I was in mid-air, before the opening of a rifle barrel, and behind me, The Argul. Then, whoosh, I was outside, on my back, mind you, looking at that orange dull fire moon with you outlined against it. It was most frightening, Crow. Something just whisked me out of my life in one spot into another."

"I know."

"You, too? Oh Crow! Who were we?"

"I am Crow and you are Plum. That must be enough."

"But it isn't."

"We are finding each other."

Plum watched the way sunlight changed colors, sliding from this leaf to that bit of wood, into that dollop of water, across that glass. "So many, many, many beauties," she said. "More than one can take in."

"Always there's more beauty than one can take in. Come. Let us look." He flapped away and she flew after him, then beside him, heading north. They crossed a river, flew over three hills, floated down to see houses hidden among the trees, porches where charms and chimes and plants hung from beams, where wooden barrels along paths caught rainwater. Crossed another river to the west, then back, over the school, factory, courthouse, two humble homes.

Late afternoon, the air cooler, they alighted at their home.

"Where is the Mississippi?" Plum thought.

"We'll know if we need to," Crow answered. "It's evening. Time to rest, sleep."

"And then we'll have more work to do?"

"Yes. Perhaps here."

Plum looked again at the house. "I do love them."

"Yes. So do we all. Love."

She tilted her eyes up, acknowledging the depth of their friendship. "We will have more adventures, won't we?"

Crow shuddered his wings, stretched his neck, pointed his beak to the sky and made a clear bell note, so beautiful. "I don't know."

Plum retired into her hollow. Crow rested outside her door, as was his habit, adoring the goodness of her fine and feisty self. A thought came to him that was his own, his very own, and he gave it utterance that might have sounded like "Caw" to most, but to him, and to the wee woman who knew him best, opened up worlds: "Ye asks who be we? Eee'm nae surra, boot methinks eee ahm nae crow and ye arrh nae weetch."

"Theen wha? Wha ahm eee, Crow? Wha ahm eee?"

"An ahngel, methinks. Surraly. Moost surraly. Thee est une loovly ahngel."

A CHOICE TIME

$\mathcal{D}$raping strands of mistletoe and holly now served as curtain at Plum's door.

"How did you hang them?" she asked.

"With my beak and my will."

"Clever Crow."

Crow deposited gifts just inside the entry to Plum's abode—bits of cotton and patches of fabric, foam, strips and wee blocks of wood, some of which were so fresh they might have been taken from a store or through a briefly open window.

"You are making me a nest," Plum said. "Should you make one for yourself?"

"No. I need none. I'm feathered and hardy."

"Feathers can't be enough protection in snow and ice."

"Have you experienced snow and ice?"

"I believe not."

"Neither have I," Crow said, "but my nature guides me, and I think the pine tree would be the best shelter."

Plum hadn't thought that he might shelter away from her. "Could you show me a nest? An empty one."

"Why?"

"I can't imagine one being suitable for you. Neither large enough nor comfortable."

He dipped his head closer, a glint in his black eyes. "You would have me be comfortable?"

"Yes. I would help make it so. Within reason."

"Within reason, of course."

He led her into the shadows under the pine boughs, where a nest of interwoven twigs hung like a deep basket between two branches.

Plum immediately thought the nest crude, jagged and jutting and impossible for him.

"It's old now," Crow said, "but it was softly lined with grass and feathers, perfect for a crow, though no male crow nests alone." He stepped into the nest, legs folding beneath him, his head erect, his beak a little over one edge, and his long, lovely tail feathers extending past the opposite edge. "I fit."

"It's like a boat for one sailor," Plum asserted. Crow looked natural there, and yet she was dismayed. She whirled around to locate where the plum tree was. Not far. But still separate. She turned back. The boughs were swaying from a breeze and the blackness of Crow fled and reappeared, like flickers of him that might fade away.

"Oh Crow. If you must have a nest, I will help you build one. Perhaps in the plum tree?"

"I want none and need none, just your understanding. The nest is not rough and ugly to a crow. Even you might be comfortable."

Plum considered the long boughs, the thousands of needle leaves that could catch and sluice away rain and sleet. She glanced at Crow, his silky, fleeting shadow. "If you were there." Plum said. "To be sure."

He rumbled softly, stood, stepped to the branch. He

offered his wing, and Plum climbed up, fingers weaving with the soft feathers. He leapt and lifted.

"Do you hear that melody, Crow? It follows us."

"Yes, I hear it, but I think we hear the wind and we make it a song."

"It must be important."

"I agree. Everything we do is. We make the world."

She dreaded returning to their branch for fear he would leave her, but he sidewalked a short distance on the branch and sat. Uneasy and unready to give up the night, Plum brushed aside the vines, their scent flowing around her and into the tree. She disrobed to pantaloons and camisole, lay on her bed thinking of all the comforts Crow had tried to give her. All the flights they had taken. He was with her from the first day—and from before. They were meant to be together. Unless separating was a part of their fate! Having to part over and over! She leapt from the fluffy bed and ran, thrusting herself through the vines. "Crow!"

"Here."

"I thought you might have gone."

"Never far. I can hear your voice wherever I be."

She ran lightly to him. "We have been guided constantly. Wouldn't you agree?"

"I don't disagree."

Plum pointed to the yard below, now bearing leaves and twigs as well as sprigs of dry grass. "Remember when you danced around me, to urge me to fly, to know what I already knew? We must do it again, only both of us."

She darted to the ground, motioning him to join her, which he did, his wings whispering the air and stirring an audience of leaves.

Plum moved backward till she could see the full height of him. Such a bold and handsome Crow. "We must do a circle round," she said. "Three of them together. It must be three."

"And then?"

"I don't know. You often don't know and yet you continue on."

"True."

"And we must look at each other and want to know, really want to know who we were."

Crow gazed at her intently, then lowered his head.

"Crow!"

He raised up. "Would you have us leave the children?"

"Never. We'll be here. We may have always been here."

"That could be."

Plum breathed deeply, briefly lay her hand over her heart, then looked at Crow. "I'll begin from here and you from there, going in opposite directions. We must sing. We will pass each other twice and the third time we meet we will stop."

She hummed the familiar melody, turned to her left. "Now."

They sang, alternately walking, flying, hovering, lighting to hold equal distance, eyes on one another, hearts open.

A circle round, a circle round, a circle round must be.
To find true love, to find true love, to find true love, find me.
Once.

A circle round, a circle round, a circle round must be.
To find true love, to find true love, to find true love, find me.
Twice.

Plum and Crow ceased movement, their thoughts intertwining. They were on the precipice of knowing and of leaving. A circle round remained. Were they ready? Dare they risk leaving the children? Dare they lose the mystery?

A choice!

The world held its breath.

They both shot into the air, meeting in the center of the circle, Crow turning so Plum could alight on his back, then rising toward the yellow moon, across the deep blue, over tree tops, elated, both of them, filled with hope and love for each other and every living thing. This was their world for now, for however long it had to be. The moon seemed most familiar, as if it had never changed, was their special guardian and could hold them in a frame whenever they might part so they could come again. Crow flapped slowly, dipped, flapped up. Clouds swam across the heavens. The night wind sang.

NOTES ON PLUM AND CROW

When I was a child, my mother told me that God was in charge, that he was powerful and good, and that anything he made large he could make smaller. Creatures could be infinitesimally tiny. There was more in the world around us and beyond than we could see, and certainly more than we could understand. She set my imagination free, and encouraged open-mindedness to the possibilities of worlds, not just mine. There was a witch at Taskee Junction. The Indians in the north part of the state had a healing stone. Crows were clever and gave warning. Birds saved children. Ghosts visited. And will-o-the-wisps sometimes got in the car with a person and rode for a while. Fairies, birds, turtles, squirrels, volunteer trees, warrior bluejays, flowers, stones, songs, everything was important in some way, a bit of magic. That kind of world is in my past, and my present. I see grand battles on a small scale in the world around. I follow the characters in my quiet moments and their doings are always important. Plum and Crow came as a pair years ago, and finally I know most of their story. They're real to me and I hope they will be to readers as well.

ACKNOWLEDGMENTS

Special thanks to Michael Hobbs and Audrey Martin for their reading and guidance in capturing the world of Plum and Crow. My thanks also to the members of Blackwater Literary Society for their patience and indulgence in my pursuit of this story. And, as has been true all my career, my deepest gratitude to my daughter Kristine Lowe-Martin for her sharp expertise and her compassionate nature.

ABOUT THE AUTHOR

R. M. Kinder, aka B.A.L. McMillan, is a Missouri writer publishing through both traditional and indie presses. Her fiction spans realism and fantasy in different genres. She is the author of five novels, three collections of short stories, and a dual media biography of a Missouri fiddler. Her short story collections have received the Willa Cather Award by Helicon Nine Press; the University of Michigan Award for Literary Fiction; and the University of Notre Dame Creative Writing Program's Richard Sullivan Award. She lives in Warrensburg, Missouri with her husband, Baird, pets Lark and Pip, many backyard creatures, and from where she works with small presses to promote regional writing.

Web site: http://www.rmkinder.net

Blog: http://rmkinder.wordpress.com

ALSO BY R.M. KINDER

An Absolute Gentleman

A Cat for All Seasons

A Common Person and Other Stories

Ghost House

A Near Perfect Gift and Other Stories

Old-Time Fiddling: Hal Sappington, Missouri Fiddler

Sweet Angel Band and Other Stories

Tune of Murder (writing as B.A.L. McMillan)

The Universe Playing Strings